CW00968849

1A19 £2.49

DROWN

DROWN

A TWISTED TAKE ON
THE CLASSIC FAIRY TALE

ESTHER DALSENO

First Edition published in Berlin, Germany in September 2015 by 3 Little Birds Books

1

A CIP catalogue record of this book is available from the Deutsche National Bibliothek

ISBN 978-3-00-050540-9

3 Little Birds Books
Libanonstrasse 85
70186 Germany

For Florence Finch,
little love of my life.

PROLOGUE

I T WAS DESTINED to fail because it was an artificial species. It was nothing but a whisper in the dark, a smear upon the perfect page of humankind, some skeletal thing that has long since corroded in the closet. Little pieces of it swept away with the breeze every time the door opened. Of course you know the story, didn't we all? We all read about it as children, and didn't all the little girls flock to the movie houses when a bigtime studio produced a version of it, a happy, sappy, songs-and-talking-animals sort of ordeal? We sucked the marrow out of it, and the bones just drifted away with the tide.

It came about, of course, because of the wrath of a woman.

The rumour was to blame. A commonplace, folklore rumour typical to a fishing village settled on the coast of one of the world's most unpredictable seas. That rumour still exists and hardly in this town alone. It is written on the face of every person you have ever met, in the subtext of every book you've ever read. It is the hope of every unhappy person. Right now, it is on the tip of your tongue.

There was once a woman whose heart broke in two. She had been carrying a basket of tomatoes, ordinary tomatoes so swollen and red it almost seemed like they too were beating. She was carrying the basket to her husband, who loved these tomatoes, who also loved her. Her own husband, who was ill in bed and required soup. They lived in the lighthouse, and this lighthouse thought it had seen everything. It was so old and venerable, so esteemed by the wind that howled at its throat, so adored by the waves that crashed at its feet. It thought that nothing had the power to surprise anymore, but how foolish we are in our pride!

The woman ran down the pier, and the gales screamed their warning. As she flung open the door, birds of the air swooped down on her in foreboding. The ocean roared as she alighted the stairs. Every raindrop wept for her. Even the molecules in the atmosphere slowed time for her, giving her micro-chances to turn back. But as she pushed open the bedchamber door, lightening illuminated the room in sorry resignation.

And then the woman with a heart like a swollen red tomato beheld the sticky cobweb of limbs entwined upon her own bed. She dropped the basket. She ran away as fast as she could, because both sides of her ribcage were ramming together now in battle, and she could feel her very bones crack and cry out from the pain. And in the black blur that always proceeds the moment when a heart splinters in two, she remembered that she had once heard a rumour, and it could save her from this condition.

If she were a rational woman, she might have reconsidered. She could have wept and banged her fists against the rocks and wailed and rocked like a baby, without her mother's arms. She could have returned to the lighthouse, and in the presence of her husband, made demands and delivered ultimatums. Resolved, she could have slept by his side that night, shivering as he snored beside her, a careless arm flung over her body. Every night thence she could have replayed his excuses, his explanations, until they grew so frayed at the seams that she would have to sew them up with her own rationalities. She could have cooked his every meal. She could have raised his children to respect him, ignoring the black bile that seeped from her heart, the heart so dark now, like a shadowy dog. And when he died, she could have looked down on his withered body and laughed at the bittersweet taste of a life gone to waste. However, she was not a rational woman, and she did not reconsider.

Instead, she got in a boat. The battle of the wind and seas hardly perturbed her as she pulled the oars in a fury. The lighthouse watched as she rowed for miles out to sea, so far out that she escaped the realm of its light. For two days she rowed, not feeling her thirst, barely registering her fatigue, because the splinters of her heart dug into her will and forced her on. Then, on the final night, her sorry limbs bathed in the milk of the moon, she slipped over the edge of the boat and began to sink.

She sank. She fell below, down past the depths, past

all water, down to where the ocean ends and earth begins again - the barren place. She did not drown. She fell to the core of the earth, where there is no place further to fall into, a place where time no longer exists. And it was there she met the beings, and she realised the rumours were true.

They approached her there in the darkness, one by one in single file, yet they were an enormous united body. They asked her questions in their voices, in their single unanimous voice, in a language she began to understand.

"We are the past and the future," they declared. "We are bid to receive the ones that seek us, and grant their heart's desire. But beware your heart's desire, for those that seek us hide broken hearts, and broken hearts are divided. They will lie to you, they will deceive you."

The woman looked at her heart in all of its fragments. Its voice was clear and true as it reminded her of the injustices done to it. Nothing so forlorn and broken could lie to her – could it? However, the woman was not a rational woman, and did not heed the beings' warning. "Strip my humanity away, that I may never again walk in the race of men," was her one wish.

The beings withdrew from her and she was left in the darkness. It is impossible to tell you how long. But from time to time, she could hear their sole, unanimous whisper and knew they were undecided. Finally, after what seemed like a split-second eternity, they returned. "We are not God that we can fulfil this request," they said, and waited.

The woman was confused, for the rumour had misled her with its reports of unlimited power. She wondered who bid them, and why they spoke of God. She wondered if they were servants of the Devil. But her heart told her that none of them existed at all.

"We are merely spirits of water and air," the beings explained.

"Then I wish to die," resolved the woman, angry now that she had not done so in their pursuit in the first place.

"If you were destined to die, then indeed you would have drowned. Yet here you are, and the life inside you must be born."

She was not surprised, for she did suspect – after all, a woman is a woman, and if a woman knows anything, it is her own body. "I wish you to take it away. I wish to never see its face, and the face of my love looking back at me."

The beings were not surprised, nor did they blink their eye. They gazed upon her solemnly and declared, "We will not do what you ask. Our power lies not in life and death, and our jurisdiction is transformation. But we are wise and we have a solution, we are crafty and we will make you a bargain concerning the child."

And so the woman began to listen, and to accept, and to finally feel a cold jubilance at the promise of their words. She was granted, in part, her wish – for human blood runs too far and too deep to be erased in its entirety. She began a new life, deep below the surface of the earth, in a part-human form, and thus began the race of merfolk.

Years passed, of which she dwelt in the depths furthest away from the light of the sun. Slowly, she began to create this race out of what remained within her, and the people were cold blooded, long-lived, and possessing each a heart that did not beat.

I should tell you that the lighthouse, when it heard the sad tale of this woman, was so surprised it began to weep. Tears of brick and stone it shed, all falling in great, deadly slabs. It was such a colossal structure that when it was finally reduced to rubble and dust, it realised it had swallowed the entire village, and not one life remained.

ONE
THE LITTLE MERMAID

"NANNY, HOW LONG will I live?"

"Three hundred years."

"How about three hundred years and one day?"

"No, my dear."

"Two hundred years, three hundred and sixty-four days?"

"No, my pet."

"But why –"

"Hush now, my sweet."

The old woman looked at her charge and felt that cloudy confusion that often accompanied the King's youngest daughter. This young thing was not like the other six princesses. Her face was different. Often, her mouth would turn up at the corners and her eyes would shine, glisten, like she knew a secret. It was haunting. Something about it turned her blood to ice, just for an instant.

"Nanny, how old am I?"

"You're twelve."

"How old are you?"

"Two hundred and sixty."

"So you will die soon."

"Yes, I will."

The little mermaid's expression darkened a fraction. It was her face that often disturbed the other folk. It would change, and change suddenly. It would twist and contort. It would evoke the shadow of a thing that the merfolk forgot they knew. It hurt them. And strangely, the little mermaid understood this and often would regulate her expression, and keep her mouth pursed and her eyes blank and her brow straight. She didn't like the way the others looked at her.

"Nanny, why do we live so long and human beings so short?"

"Because of the Great Condition."

"What is the Great Condition?"

"It is the disease that shortens human lives."

"But what is it called?"

"It's called heartbreak."

A silence like a chasm lay between them.

"What's heartbreak?" asked the mermaid, a little afraid.

"I don't know," replied her nanny.

After a time, the little mermaid grew bored and swam away. Her fat little tail stung in the salt water, and she didn't like the way her hair always fell in her eyes. Clotted brown blood congealed along her silver fins, for she had had an accident a few days earlier. She just wasn't as agile as her sisters. The currents kept on surprising her, ramming her into the seedy coral that formed the palace. But it was not a complete loss. Her broken scales had been carefully scraped off the walls and sold for one year's supply of food. Her father had even thanked her. Then he'd made a comment that she alone had kept the royal family in luxury for the past twelve years. She didn't understand. It made her feel deflated.

She was itching again. When she was alone, she often scratched at her gills with her fingernails, leaving her neck red and pulsating. Her nanny would often chide her for it, reminding her that it was not beautiful. However, the little mermaid often dreamed that they did not belong there. She was tired of beauty. She didn't know why it exhausted her so much. Everywhere she looked, the world glittered and shone. There were lights all over the place. Even when she slept, lights flickered under her eyelids. She longed for darkness and drabness.

The distinct awareness that she was somehow less valuable than her sisters often hovered in the back of her mind. Their reflections in the looking-glass were different too. The little mermaid was too young yet to realise why, but she knew that she was not as pretty as they. They were radiant and cold, with skin so white you could see the black veins underneath. Every cell on their bodies glimmered in the lights, but their irises never fluctuated. Their posture was perfect, their bodies held erect always, their silver tails coiling against the current like Chinese serpents. Their hair was never in their eyes, and they never scraped their tails against coral. They were so beautiful that they parted crowds of common folk, and ventured nowhere without their guardians, who prevented the folk from reaching out to pluck a single strand of royal hair. It was said one strand could buy housing for the gypsy folk, who travelled in groups all over the ocean, causing strife and chaos.

She'd seen a gypsy once. He was lurking inside the palace gates, and she was watching from a window. She had just awoken from a nightmare and imagined she were still inside of it – for he was a sight unlike anything she had ever seen. His back was broken. His cancerous tail alone bore his slight weight, so cracked and dry it appeared, with many great growths all over. His hands were mere stumps, fingers long sawn off, the skin around the knuckles corroding with barnacles. His face was alarming – his head shorn with one lashless eye peering at her. It wasn't long before the guardians came upon him and slit his throat. The blood drifted away from his lifeless body, thick like tar. She had remained in her chamber the next day, because she could not stop shuddering.

She was so disturbed that she summoned all her courage to encroach her sisters about it. They, in recent years, had taken a disliking to her questions and often did not answer them at all. They never explained why. They often looked at her with their great, empty eyes with something that could have been astonishment, if merfolk were capable of astonishment, that is.

"He wanted to kill you, of course," said one sister.

"But why?"

The sisters looked at each other, examining each other, as if they answer lay between them. "Because you are beautiful."

"You are so beautiful that your body could buy a whole kingdom. But they are ugly. They are so ugly that they are poor. They have nothing to eat. Not like us. We are so beautiful that we eat all day. We are so beautiful that one of our scales is worth one hundred million of theirs."

"But they wanted to kill me. That's wrong!" the little mermaid passionately exclaimed.

The sisters were confounded. "Wrong? Why is this wrong? He was hungry and had to eat. To eat, he had to kill you. This is not wrong, it is right."

"I am so beautiful I could buy the whole world!" proclaimed the eldest princess, who did not notice how distraught the youngest sister had become.

Thus the little mermaid learned her world's greatest paradox: that their currency was beauty, and their coin was body parts. And she also remembered that even though her beauty could buy a kingdom, her sister's could buy the whole world.

Today was a special day and even the currents were electric. It was the third princesses' birthday and she was undertaking preparations to rise to the surface for the first time. It was tradition that the royal children behold the human world on their most momentous birthday. The sacred rite of passage must be endured alone, without protection. Thereafter, the mermaids could return to the surface as they pleased.

The common merfolk came and went from the water's surface without limits. Some of the poorer children accompanied their mothers, riding on their backs, gleaning shrimp from amongst the froth. Idle folk frolicked in the waves, spying on sailors and mocking them. The unlucky ones were captured, some living short lives at the mercy of an oddities collector, travelling the land in tanks with such polluted water that they would quickly drown. Still others were mercilessly butchered and sold at high prices as delicacies to the rich, who questioned the fabled origins of the meat, but could not deny its sumptuous flavour.

The third princess need not have been apprehensive about the coming evening, for a unique and highly expensive spell had been purchased to fortify her. The Sea King himself had forged an alliance with the Finfolk, a subdued and artful race of merpeople that dwelt in the red caves close to the gorge. Currency and beauty they had not, and yet every part of their bodies remained intact, due to the old magic that was rumoured to dwell under the gorge. The potion had been brewed to perfection, and contained ingredients so horrible that they cannot be mentioned here. However, the Sea King himself asked no questions, and the princess swallowed it without second thought.

The sisters had been forbidden to venture near the red caves, although curiosity to do so, they did not possess. It was rumoured that once in a while, a human body was sucked into the abyss.

Many years ago, the eldest had witnessed a human body drown. She said it had been a wondrous thing when the human had finally died, for its body then simply wafted with the tide, like a feather drifting down to earth. All the sisters had then murmured in response all sorts of dreary opinions, especially the common belief that humans only became beautiful once they had died. But the creature that lived secretly in little mermaid's deepest cavity, within her chest, began to drum furiously. She succumbed to the twisting pain in her gut and lunged at her oldest sister, teeth and fists and fingernails flaying.

Later that day, the little mermaid lay on the cold floor of her chamber, powerless over her body that was heaving and choking her. Her face was screwed up in pain and her eyes burned. She didn't know why, but she felt such a tightness inside of her, a tightness that wanted to explode into a red rage. There was heaviness too, something that wanted to embed her into the floor and never let her rise again. But the strangest thing of all was a feeling called remorse, as she remembered the alarmed look in her sister's eyes, and her flesh under her nails.

She suddenly became aware of a shadow that lingered in the doorway. It was the eldest princess. The little mermaid turned her face to her and wailed, "Why didn't you save him?"

The eldest princess was silent for a long time, because it took her a long time to find the answer. "It never once occurred to me."

Then, little mermaid, filled with pity, reached out her arms in embrace, but her sister became afraid and fled.

The occasion was not mentioned again, and the eldest princess had resumed her relationship with the youngest as if nothing had happened, partly because mermaid's memories are short, and partly because the princess did not know how to change.

And now, many years later, the little mermaid watched as the third-eldest princess was attended to by the servants, ornaments of rich oyster and pearl attached to her body, in preparation for the surfacing ahead. The other mermaids watched solemnly as the debutante's appearance began to change under the power of the spell. Her fiery scales began to bleach out, her skin lost its radiance, and her hair discharged its lustre and became like the sea-weed that grew unfettered along the wastelands. It seemed to all present that a smell manifested from the princess, an aroma impressing upon them images of rotting carcasses and old blood. In fact, she became a sight so foreign and spectral, that commoners were repelled by her. But to the little mermaid, she had never looked so well, and smelled of what she imagined land-corals to be like.

The little mermaid spent the rest of the day restless and anxious, as was normal whenever a sister surfaced. She replayed in her mind all of the sights her sisters had relayed over the years, and used her limited imagination to conjure pictures of them. She imagined icebergs monstrous and deadly, and snow, and what it would feel like to shiver. She imagined mountains and hills, and that furry green substance that grew all over the land. She imagined little children, all rolling about in the waves with their twisted faces. She imagined the little brown animals that often accompanied them, wagging their back appendages and omitting short, gruff noises. And she imagined the land-fish, fish with fins so large and powerful it carried them into the air.

Hours later, when the spell had worn off, the third sister returned to the palace. The princesses gathered around her as her scales regained their glorious splendour, and her skin glowed white and luminescent once more. They nodded their heads gravely at her news, like wise old souls who had seen everything.

"The ocean was angry," said the third-eldest, "and the waves were trying to eat each other. They tossed the ships about like they were weightless. The human beings ran and made loud sounds. But the sky opened up and sent flashes of light, and then water fell from it."

"Did you see the humans? What did they look like?" asked the little mermaid.

"They all look the same, two arms, two legs."

"But what about their faces? What about their eyes?"

"We all have a face," said the third-eldest. "We all have eyes. Even the fishes and the octopi have eyes."

"But they are different!" exclaimed the little mermaid. "Surely they must be different!"

"We are all the same," said the eldest daughter, who had seen the most of the world.

"If we are all the same, then why can't we die of heartbreak?"

The sisters looked at each other in confusion. "Heart-break?" they repeated to each other, and shrugged. "Human weakness," they concluded. "They are not as strong as we."

"What happens to the humans when they die?" asked the little mermaid.

"They go into the ground, as we go into the sea," replied the sister who had seen a funeral procession.

But this was not the answer the youngest was prepared for. "Not their bodies," she clarified, "the other thing."

There was a silence, and the sisters seemed reluctant to respond. Finally, "What other thing?" one asked.

"The thing that lives inside them."

The sisters began to talk amongst themselves, suggesting solutions like parasites and leeches. After much discussion, they turned to the youngest and said, "It dies with them, of course."

But the little mermaid was shaking her head. "It doesn't. I know it doesn't."

That night, when the little mermaid sank into sleep, she dreamed that there was someone outside, watching her from the window. All around the person's sunken face swirled transparent hair, like thin rice noodles. And its eyes were opaque and milky, with no pupil.

Two
OF THE SEA WITCH

NOW THE OLD Sea King was a venerable creature, feared for his power and influence, and respected by all his subjects. They paid homage to him and spoke truthfully of his honour, beauty and might. His authority had never been challenged, for no one in the kingdom possessed an ounce of his strength. In fact, mutiny and envy did not exist in the watery world, and through their rapid evolution, the merfolk were left with animal instincts and sentiments such as territorialism, anger and a vague sense of curiosity. All other humane characteristics had been bred out of the species, and citizens simply fulfilled their roles as their fathers had, as did their fathers before them.

The Sea King had inherited the throne later in life, and only then did he take a wife. After some long years, she fell pregnant and three months later she retired to the birthing chamber and laid a single egg. The Sea King was curious about the egg, as he had yet to behold the miracle of birth, and took to visiting the birthing chamber every so often to watch the egg, and the life inside it evolve. Fingers of wonder and magic would touch his consciousness, and he would reach out his hand and caress the membranous shell containing his child.

It gave him an odd sensation as the jelly-like ovum wobbled beneath his touch. He meticulously examined the way tiny blue veins skirted the outer circuits of the egg, all journeying to the icy grey foetus, pumping nourishment into the child. He could barely make out the shadow of the living thing, but he would imagine it, rotating in the waters of its sanctuary, white skin stretching over its small bones, each and every sparkling scale forming on the frail fins. If the Sea King knew this word, he would have described the experience as 'holy', as over the nine months of incubation, he guarded and monitored the genesis of his first child.

Finally, the female inhabitants of the palace, including the Queen and the newly-acquired nanny, confirmed that it was Time. Together they descended to the depths of the birthing chamber. Hours they waited, as the egg would occasionally quiver, then fall asleep again. Finally, a soft rumble emerged from the gamete and it began to quake violently. Huge tears appeared in the thick, pulsing membrane, and sticky ooze excreted from the rapidly deflating ovum. Finally, a small hard blob flew from its cell, and landed unceremoniously upon the floor. As the egg's remnants evaporated in a sickly steam, all eyes watched the little knot of matter, as it lay like a dead thing.

The Sea King began to feel alarm but it was

unnecessary, for after a few moments, the blob began to rise with the current and struggle in the water. From the hard grey pod, a pearly, gleaming tail emerged and weakly kicked against the water. A little white fist broke through the husk, and along with it, all the other parts that make up a merchild's body. Discarding its final prison, the King's eldest daughter flew upon the Queen's full breasts, and fed like a ravenous, dying creature.

For two years, the child was nourished by her mother, until her fins grew strong and her teeth brittle enough to tear through flesh. By that time, the second princess had been born, and their mother was pregnant with another egg. For six years, the noble queen produced daughters, all precisely one year apart, and the King was pleased, because he had selected her upon the promise of her fertility. After these exhausting years, the Queen's beauty was slowly sucked out of her and siphoned into the bodies of her daughters. Her breasts were empty and sagging, her womb stiff as cardboard.

As mentioned earlier, merfolk live for three hundred years precisely, if they are not hunted and slaughtered. The Sea King's ancestors had been such successful negotiators that the entire ocean respected the law and rule of merfolk, and large predators refrained from attacking or consuming any citizens. In fact, sea creatures tried to avoid the mer-folk as much as possible – for to them, the species was too much human for their liking, and far too little fish. There was something nasty about the merfolk, they decided. Even though they appreciated that the merpeople did not meddle in the natural order of things, they felt uneasy in their territory, and they suspected it had something to do with the things that lived under the gorge.

Being a peaceful race, and a race that did not practice violence unless killing for food, the merfolk had one major predator: themselves. As intelligent beings, they were mainly cautious when surfacing, and did not tempt fate by drawing human attention. Merfolk were unsure how old their race was, and they assumed they had existed from the very origins of earth, as all species do. But the sad truth was that in the short generations since they were created, sea creatures began to avoid merfolk increasingly as the race evolved to stranger and stranger heights. Large shoals of fish no longer passed over the populated parts of the reef, choosing instead the route over the wastelands. Octopus and ray also avoided these areas, because the great pale orbs of light that were erected all over the kingdom stung their eyes. These days, food was difficult to find, and prices became higher, causing the poor to kill cold-bloodedly for items to trade for their food.

It came as a great surprise to the kingdom when, after the birth of the sixth royal princess, the Queen disappeared. It was certain she had not been murdered, as anyone who had seen her lately knew she wasn't worth a red herring. The princesses told themselves that she had gone to the land, and would return when the time was right. But the Sea King knew she was dead.

When mermaids die, they are not buried. Their flesh does not loosen from their bones and slowly decay. Instead, they instantly dissolve and become sea-foam, riding on the crust of the waves. In the rare occurrence that they die on land, their bodies become the mist that settles on the ocean. The Sea King did not know how she died, nor did he trouble his mind with theories or possibilities, as that was not his way.

He was a good King, and a good father, and it did not concern him that he produced no male lineage, for in that world, no gender was valued higher than the other. As any parent in the animal kingdom, he was fiercely protective of his own. But even the animal kingdom has glitches.

Merfolk mate for life, and love-making was not for any other purpose than to produce offspring. This is why the Sea King was perturbed when he discovered hot desires were directed toward a particular female he had once encountered, but had never seen again. There were rumours about this woman, and because merfolk do not question information, they were widely believed to be truthful. She was known to be a witch, a conjurer of powerful spells, but spells for freaks and outcasts. The wishes she granted were against nature. Those desperate enough to seek her help were never found again, and so it was assumed she practiced cannibalism. There was only one rumour that was completely accurate – that she was the most beautiful creature in the kingdom.

She lived beyond the borders of the kingdom, so deep below that all was in darkness, save for the light of the skeletal torch-fish, who sifted through the murky currents for bits of stray plankton. It was this place that the larger predators refused to frequent, and no sea-plant wished to thrive. It was believed that the witch was self-sustaining, for no nourishment was to be found in this part of the ocean.

The King recalled the last time he had seen the witch, and the memory was so vivid and fresh in his mind, it was like it was yesterday. In truth, the King had last seen her one hundred years ago, when she had sent him a message asking him to call upon her.

Now merfolk did not possess human pride, this was bred out of them in the earliest days. Neither did disloyalty, jealousy or guile exist, and if a King is asked to visit any subject of his realm, the King has no reason not to do so. As he and his guardians carefully descended to the deepest pit of the sea, he felt no anticipation for the coming event, and no sense of wonder or curiosity for the person in question. Therefore, it was a great surprise to him that suddenly, in the oily blackness, three very white and ghostly females appeared. They appeared to be hovering in the still, silent water and stared at him with their bewitching eyes, and when they opened their mouths, their words chanted in unison. Bewitching, musical unison.

> *"Be warned o King who enters here*
> *The earth and water part*
> *For the one who watches near*
> *Will grasp your beatless heart."*

The King did not understand them, for he was distracted by their sudden appearance, and his ears were not accustomed to the melody of such voices. They turned away, as if made of one body, and holding three glowing lanterns between them, began to lead him to their mistress.

Illuminated from the weak light of the lanterns, the King studied his new companions. They were white, whiter even than the complexions of his daughters, but this whiteness spread to every inch of their bodies, like a disease. The only exception was their hair, which was the palest shade of yellow, yet moving with a life force that did not emanate from the creatures. With a dull sense of horror, the King realised that entwined in that strange, colourless hair were the tentacles of great warrior jellyfish, twitching like bodies in the final throws of death, sending reluctant, dying sparks into the water; halos crowning spectres. And all over their bodies, the bleak whiteness seemed to have forgotten an identical patch on each of their lower backs, a section about the size of a coin, which was an ugly dark brown, and several black hairs sprouted from it.

They seemed to be carved out of stone for their movements were limited, as their bodies moved fluidly with the flow of the water. It was as if they were conserving all energy for a great battle. Their eyes were fringed with heavy translucent lashes, but they never blinked. Perhaps the most astonishing feature of all was their tails. At least twenty feet long, their stark yet sinuous tails curled and writhed like eels, and ended with a single point, like the far end of a serpent. These propelled them weightlessly through the water, at a much faster pace than a mere mermaid. The King began to wonder if these creatures were any relation to his species at all.

Had it not been for the lanterns, the party would never have noticed the garden. Suddenly, the King found himself swimming over partitioned land overgrown with brown weeds, frozen still, because there was no current. It was an eerie sight, and it was only when a weed brushed against his arm that the King noticed it had a face. That they all had faces. And he thought he heard whispers too, but it was in a different language and he did not understand.

The garden stopped at the mouth of a cavern, and the ghostly females beckoned for them to enter. Inside the grey walls, there came something unexpected: absolute emptiness. There was nothing, no signs of witchcraft whatsoever. There were no shelves of ingredients lining the walls, no great cauldron for a witch to whip up a brew, and no signs of a beautiful woman: shells for decorativeness, algae-creams for skin, pearls for outings. There was no looking-glass. Instead, high above them in the turrets of the enormous ceiling were a group of torch-fish, strung together by their gills with a necklace of human hooks, still alive and casting light into the chamber. As the Sea King moved about the room, his fins brushed against something unpleasant. He looked down and beheld the floor scattered with bones. There were more than fish bones here, there was the jaw of a whale, and ribs of sharks, and other large and unrecognisable skeletons. Despite himself, the Sea King shuddered.

Suddenly a terrible sound filled the room. It was a thudding, like the thudding of a deadly drum, and it filled every ear with dread. It grew closer, inspiring fear in the King and his guardians, and even the Sirens squirmed and backed away. The King sucked in his breath as the witch entered the chamber. He felt stunned, bewildered, and the racing of all the liquids in his body drowned out the thudding that went on and on, on and on. He forgot everything he knew in that instant. He felt like he was sinking inside of her.

She was beautiful, the way the colour black is beautiful, with its sleekness and oiliness and infinite darkness. A halo of black hair surrounded her, hair so long and so priceless it was surely worth his palace and all its contents. Her black tail was the tail of the eels, similar to the Sirens, enormous and writhing and she seemed to slither in the water. Her skin was so pale it seemed as if she had never surfaced and felt the sun on her face.

"Welcome," she said, but her voice was foreign, grating on the ears.

The Sea King gathered his wits and replied, "I have come to you, as summoned, my lady."

"A long journey," she acknowledged, "and I thank you for it."

Looking at her long and hard, the Sea King asked, "Have we met before? I seem to know...your face."

The witch's mouth twisted in a way he had never beheld, although it seemed strangely familiar. It was a smile, and the King could see her teeth, sharp like a sea-serpent's. "It is possible. Many claim to have seen me, and have not yet. Many who do forget for a time. But I tell you, all merfolk behold my face, either on their day of birth, or their day of death."

And it seemed to the Sea King that all the times he peered into a looking-glass as a child, he had seen this woman's face staring back at him. "Won't you return to my kingdom?" implored the King. "A beautiful lady is not safe alone in these times. I will give you my protection, and a home close to my palace."

The witch looked at him with scorn. "Do not believe I am subject to your Majesty, who will come and go as she is bid. I am subject to no law but myself."

And it occurred to him that she had once not bowed to him nor paid him homage. She had treated him like a commoner. And instead of indignation, the King felt nothing. On and on the drumming pounded. "And now you see me, do you think thieves or murderers would dare touch me?" she spread her arms out, as if in challenge.

"But surely, you should be among others, a husband, perhaps?"

The witch bared her teeth at the word. "*Husband?*" she hissed. "For what? To bear children, to bring more of *myself* into this world? There can only be one *I*," she declared, "and if I perish, I will bring your people with me."

Aware that she was frightening her guests, her tone softened and her eyes lost its hard brilliance. "But I am not alone. I have my Sirens, my beauties, who bring me stories and good tidings." Her enormous tail stretched out and interlocked itself with one of the Siren's, who purred in pleasure as it stroked her own.

"Will your Majesty play a game?" the witch asked, and in her hand appeared a flat slab of stone, painted in bright colours, with marble markers sitting upon it.

"I do not know this game," replied the King, warily.

"It is simple," remarked the witch airily, "a child's game. I shall teach you."

"And the stakes?" asked the King.

The witch feigned indifference. "No stakes. A game between friends."

"It is decreed that no game is to be played without stakes or rewards," recited the King, whose own father made the law.

The witch smiled again, and her red tongue ran heavily over her pointed teeth. "My most precious possession," she said, "for your most precious possession."

"My kingdom," realised the King. "And you?"

"My most powerful spell," said the witch.

"Agreed," said the King foolishly, for he had never yet lost a game, as his cunning was great.

The game was played for a limitless time – for time did not exist inside the witch's cavern. The pounding sound was incessant, and often it distracted the King. He felt he was losing, because his understanding of the game was slipping away with every move, and even the simplest of strategies became confused and hopelessly tangled. Thus, he was greatly astonished when the witch threw down her final marker and declared, "You win."

He was still struggling to regain his wits when a Siren produced an object out of thin air and handed it to the King. It was pulsating, like an internal organ, and was a dull orange colour. It did not look powerful or valuable at all.

"It is not yet ready," the witch explained. "The spell will grow with time, and will bloom in your darkest hour. After today, you will hide the potion, and you will forget its existence until that time. Then, you should swallow it whole and your entire fortune will change. I promise you."

The King examined the object with suspicion, which displeased the witch. "It is no trifle you hold in your hand," she warned, "for it is worth the blood of a thousand of your subjects. I have given it to you freely. I do not readily give spells where I customarily extract payment."

The King nodded gravely, and together with his guardians, left the chamber. The Sirens followed them to the edge of the garden, and proclaimed,

"You freely gave into a boon
A promise you must keep
And now you follow as a fool
The path that leads to sleep."

Unaccustomed to music, the King disregarded what little he understood of their chant and returned to his palace. Remembering the witch's face, he stowed the potion behind the looking-glass in his chamber.

True to her word, the King promptly forgot about the spell, the witch, and his visit to her. He took to the business of the Kingdom, and chose a noble maid to become his Queen. It was not until one hundred years later, when the Queen had produced six daughters and wasted away into death, that the King entered his darkest hour, and the potion behind the looking-glass began to beat out a terrible, hammering rhythm. The King was frightened by its ominous sound, and remembering the witch's words, swallowed it whole. The hard corners of the spell cut the insides of his throat as he choked it down.

Nothing happened.

Except he felt his limbs on fire, his head on fire, his dead, empty heart on fire. They were on fire for the witch, the beautiful witch, and every ounce of him ached with desire for her. For days he lumbered about, utterly consumed. Finally, when he could stand it no more, he abandoned his guardians and made a final journey to the deepest part of the sea.

THREE
THE BEGINNING
OF THE END

THE WITCH HAD not changed in the last century, there was not a single line on her face or hesitation in her movements. She appeared ageless as indeed, she was. She was spell-binding, as always, and the King was utterly bewitched. His body tingled with lust, and he was certain that the witch could see his longing etched all over his being. The Sirens were nowhere to be seen.

"I want to be with you," said the King. "I wish to mate with you urgently."

The sea-witch was filled with disgust, bile rising in her throat at the repugnance of the thought. "There is nothing that I would detest more," she declared truthfully, and turned away.

The King was taken aback, for there was no male in

existence more attractive than he, he with his glorious shining head and form so mesmerising, he so like a god. He advanced upon her, beginning a mating ritual. "You can not deny me," he said, believing it to be so, "for it is nature."

"I am not a part of your nature," responded the witch. "Have I not said I am a law unto myself?"

"I will make you my Queen," offered the King.

"You are an abomination!" spat the witch, for the very smell of him nauseated her. Yet she was prepared for this, for it was of her own design. It had taken her a hundred years to steel herself for the inevitable outcome.

The King was not discouraged and advanced further, driven by the potency of the magic within him. "I will make you my Queen, and give you half my kingdom."

The witch laughed at the absurdity of his plea. "If I had wanted your kingdom," she said scornfully, "I would have had it long ago. But who would wish to possess a realm of artificial creatures, more animal than human, who cannot *feel*, or *express*, or *hate*?"

The King did not know the meaning of these words, and so discarded them. "I will give you supremacy, and my whole kingdom. I will step down," he promised, beginning to feel desperate. He was inches away from her now, and his body had begun to coil around hers.

"Do not insult me with your paltry offerings," hissed the witch. "It was I that created your kingdom. I am the mother of all your kind. Did you not think my Sirens would report to me your every move, as they did your father's, and his father's before him? You vile creature, I witnessed your conception, and saw your malformed, artificial body in its egg. I knew your Queen and all your hideous daughters see my face in their looking-glass. You are mine, and it is *I* who grants the favours, not you."

But all of this was gibberish to the King, who, if he had the sense to listen to reason, would not fathom her words for the terrain of his intelligence was limited, and animal desire is strong. As the King began that ancient act, the witch drew in her breath and gritted her teeth. Blood began to trickle from her lip onto her chin. Her heart pounded within her, echoing in that dark cavern, but the King did not care. Every ounce of her will begged her not to throw his body off hers, to murder him and drink his blood for the outrage, the sacrilege. She had a goal, one single aspiration, and she was prepared to pay the price.

As it continued, it occurred to her that she had once enjoyed this very ritual. A face returned to her in the darkness, that loved and despised face, his body buried beneath the rubble. And in her native language that had long ago escaped her tongue and memory, she cried out his name, and the names of all the people she had known and loved. She cried out for humanity and all of its weakness. And suddenly, the King fell off her, and the spell was broken.

Filled with alarm and a faint sense of disgust, he witnessed the scene through fresh eyes and realised what he had done. His body repelled hers like magnets in reverse. His head was swimming, for had he really lain with this creature a moment ago? And why had she suddenly lost her beauty? But with one glance at the witch's contorted face, the King backed away, sensing he was in grave danger.

The witch gave into her instincts and came after him.

He had never before noticed how her nails were like long, yellow talons, and now they were embedded in his flesh and ripping it away from his bones. This time it was her own eel's tail that twisted around his own, strangling him like a snake strangles its prey. Like a ravenous wolf, her sharp teeth tore into him, and she chewed the pieces of him with relish and swallowed them with gusto. It was too easy, for her strength far outweighed his own. *Restraint, my sweet,* said her inner voice, *you must leave him alive.* Coarse, strangled cries omitted from the witch's mouth as, in an act of supreme force, the Sea King threw her off and fled.

As he longed to reach the sanctuary of the palace for the healers to begin their work, so did the Sirens attend to their mistress, who was still quivering with the heat of the fight.

The Sea King's imagination was so limited that he did not realise the trickery that lay behind the event. Still he trusted the witch's words, for he had swallowed the potion in the darkest time of his life, and the glorious reward for the witch's most valuable potion must have been that fleeting, sickly sweet hour he had lain with her. And he trusted deeply her final promise: that his entire fortune was about to change.

For the weeks that followed, the Sea King was nervous and easily alarmed, perturbed by the events that had conspired. If he had been a mortal man, he would have spent hours in self-analysis, he would have suspected the woman, he would have sulked under the burden of guilt. But merfolk know nothing of these things, and it is not in their natures to analyse or to consider, so the King went about his business as usual, with the exception of three things.

He took to avoiding his daughters regularly, refusing to spend time with them and barely listening to the nanny's report on their health and doings. When he heard their voices in the corridor, he would escape to the nearest chamber. When his eldest daughter entered the throne room uninvited on one occasion, he berated her in front of his court, and she fled from him. To him, they were an omen of bad tidings, but he did not confide this to anyone. And vaguely, they reminded him of his Queen, and if he were a mortal, he would have felt he had betrayed her, and this was unpleasant also.

He tried not to spend copious amounts of time alone, because when he did, he heard that terrible beating sound that would raise goosebumps all over his flesh. He began to fear the dark, and ordered his servants to move one of the great orbs of light, a gift from the beings long ago, into his quarters. His only solace was sleep, and if he were human, he would have been haunted by nightmares.

The third exception was that the King ordered all the looking-glasses in the palace to be destroyed. There were many complaints about this from the female staff who enjoyed their vanities, but not so much as the six princesses, who were the most beautiful in the realm and so loved to look upon themselves.

Three months passed without incident, until one day, a mysterious delivery arrived for the King. When he entered his throne room and saw it there, he was gripped with fear. He ordered it to be brought to the birthing chamber, and there it remained. The staff asked no questions of this curious event, and soon everyone forgot about the delivery and what lay in the chamber below. Everyone except the nanny, who was more maternal than other merfolk, and knew there was a child waiting to be born.

She crept down to the birthing chamber one day and peeked into the room. It was the same as always, but the water smelled stale, as if it hadn't been penetrated for months. It was the strangest egg she had ever seen. In her long career, the nanny had always worked in childbearing. She had played midwife to the larger mammals, abandoned by their mates. She had delivered eggs of the unicorn-fish. She collected the little male seahorses, stomachs bulging with their young, and studied and ways and means of insemination. But never in her experience had she seen an egg like this.

It had a brittle shell around it, glowing warm-brown like amber, as if it had been underwater for a very long time. Inside, the ovum itself was a healthy pink colour, and the foetus filled it completely, gently swaying in its cocoon of jelly. It had a large head, and a healthy body and – the nanny shuddered – no fins whatsoever. Although the amber hid it well, the nanny swore she saw legs, human legs, in the place of a fish tail. Bursting to tell the King, but knowing to do so would be to give herself up, she fled from the chamber in a hurry.

The nanny did not forget about the egg. She calculated its delivery and accordingly, its arrival, and was present the moment the child was born. She held it in her arms, a perfectly normal little mermaid, and the nanny shook her head with disbelief, for it was clear that sorcery had been at work. She knew what she saw, or at least, she thought she did. And these very fins the nanny now stroked, examining them for a sign, a clue. There was nothing. But the child was hungry and the nanny could not feed her with her own barren breasts.

After a wet-nurse had been found, the nanny set herself to the task of informing the King of the birth. She anticipated his reaction: indifference, possible displeasure, and the nanny hoped he would not reject the child, as animals often reject young that is not their own.

"Your Majesty," she said, bowing low when she found him, "the egg in the birthing chamber is hatched."

"Is it...alive?" asked the Sea King, who had wished it to die like another before him.

"Yes, your Majesty. It is a healthy baby girl."

And the King uprooted himself and made his way to the nursery, and when he saw the nursemaid feeding the little mermaid, he tore her from the breast and stared at her.

"I see," he said after a while, and returned her to the nursemaid.

After that, the King began to visit the new arrival often, and from a distance, would watch her closely for signs of himself. He started to visit the others too, and after a time became his old self again. The witch was forgotten, and so was the mysterious delivery, and the little princesses adopted their new sister immediately, and all was well once more.

She grew like her sisters, but there was something strange about her appearance, for she did not shine as brightly as they, and her movements were not the same. She was prone to clumsiness, and often injured herself on common objects. She was not as strong a swimmer, tiring quickly. Her face would transform when her sisters' remained deadpan and still. Her hair always tangled into messy reeds, and her hide was so thick you could not see her veins beneath. She scratched herself frequently, for her gills troubled her, and she was often found staring at her tail as if she didn't know what it was for. She was disobedient, wilful, and rebellious, and because no merfolk had ever seen these characteristics before, the nanny did not know what to do with her. Every time she tried to mention it to the King, he would stare at her as if she were mad. Indeed, she often wondered if she was, for the little mermaid was one of her kind in all the ways that mattered, and to deny it after all these years seemed insane.

But the child was insatiably curious, always questioning everything, until she had exhausted all around her, who could not fathom the meaning of her questions.

"Nanny, what happens when you sleep?"

"Your body rests."

"What about your mind?"

"I'm sure your mind rests too, my sweet."

"Not mine. I see pictures in my head. They say things and do things. What is it called?"

"I don't know, my dear."

"Do you see things when you sleep?"

"No."

"Does Father?"

"You will have to ask him."

And of the answers the nanny did know, she kept them to herself, for she did not want to excite the little creature, who was far too excitable as it was. Until one day, even the old woman had to acknowledge that it was time, for the little mermaid had reached her most special birthday, and was ready to surface for her rite of passage.

"Nanny, what happens to the humans when they die?"

"Their bodies rot and decay into the ground."

"What about the other thing, the thing that lives inside them?"

"Why, it lives forever, my sweet, and never dies."

The little mermaid's eyes widened and for once, she forgot to conceal her emotion. "Forever?" she squeaked. "But where? And why? And what is it called?"

The nanny flinched, but answered nonetheless. "It is called the Immortal Soul. And it lives not on earth, but in heaven."

Something was hammering inside the little mermaid's chest now, a sensation she had mostly forgotten about. "Why?" she gushed, as if she were waiting all of her life for this moment.

"The humans are the most fortunate species, because they were created by God. He breathed into them his own breath, and his own breath lives inside them, as their Immortal Souls."

The little princess closed her eyes and tried to imagine this, as she had never heard anything so glorious and beautiful in her life.

"And when their bodies die," continued the nanny, "their souls are called up to heaven itself, where God lives, and they live with him forever."

The little mermaid's wild excitement soon faded into a melancholy sadness as she realised the momentum of the old lady's words. "But if humans were created by God, who were we created by?"

"I don't think anybody knows," said the nanny.

"And we don't have Immortal Souls, do we?"

"No, my precious."

"Can we somehow get Immortal Souls?" inquired the little mermaid, although she already knew the answer.

"No, Princess. You will never have an Immortal Soul."

The little mermaid looked so downcast that hastily, the nanny stated, "But who wants an Immortal Soul when the price to pay is such a short life? We merfolk are the lucky ones, we live for three hundred long years."

The little mermaid shook her head. "I would rather live on earth for a short time if it meant heaven for eternity," she breathed, and her hope was like a prayer.

"And die of the Great Condition?" asked the Nanny. "It's a painful thing, a dreadful thing, and you could not bear it."

"Oh, to die of heartbreak!" exclaimed the mermaid passionately.

"You will never die of heartbreak," predicted the Nanny dryly.

Four

A PRINCE

IT WAS LONELY at the top. That was the little mermaid's first impression as her head crashed through the last watery layer – the final frontier between all she was and all she hoped for.

She had expected the human world to be chaotic – a mixed bag of screeches and howls and crashes and voices – anything but this silence that was so like yet unlike her world below. It was lonesome too and she felt a crashing disappointment, for in her naivety she had expected something different, like this new world had waited for her so desperately that it would send out a host of friends to welcome her. But there was nothing except this whiteness, this bright pain that filled her eyes. She wondered if she had been lied to all along, and there was nothing beyond the surface, just emptiness. But she waited in the waves and through the white silence, something appeared.

It was a flying fish. It soared above her head, squawking, then dove beneath the surface, clacking its beak hungrily. The little mermaid watched in awe as it arose, its magnificent wings spread, and flew to heaven. As she watched it disappear into a red, round sphere of light, it seemed to her that she had just witnessed a departed Immortal Soul returning to God, its maker. And it occurred to her that this God could be none other than the great red light overhead. It was so bright that she could not directly look upon it, such was its glory. And when her eyes screwed up tight, she saw imprints of God in the darkness beneath her lids. When she looked away, she felt the God all around her, its rays stroking her skin and filling her heart with thick, hot soup. It seemed to her that she had been frozen all of her life and was slowly thawing.

Now that she was looking harder, she noticed that everything the God touched turned to magic – for she could see a landscape dancing in the distance, and wonderful pillars of rock on the shore, and the greenness of fauna, and the moving images of little living creatures running up and down the beach. She could even see its reflection in the sea itself, and her own reflection beside it, and she realised then that God had wanted her here all along, and they were destined to meet one day in the heavens.

Gladness filled her, and she saw the sky was streaked with orange and pink, and the fading brightness of all around her. She was aware that the brightness was not the same as that below, where everything glittered and shone so brittle and hard. Instead, this light spread all over the world, like a layer of film, and the occupants of earth could *breathe*. And breathe she did now, taking greedy gulps of salty air. She felt that the human beings were the luckiest creatures indeed, not for their possession of their immortal souls, but that they could fill their nostrils with this goodness and feel God on their faces.

The God was going to sleep now, for half of it was buried in the ocean, but the little mermaid was not sad because she knew that she would see it again. Time ticked by, and she did not move, and when the God was fast asleep, she saw its angels emerge in the sky and wink down at her, thousands of them.

But then, across the waves, came a sound that entered her ears and vibrated through her, cutting her into jagged pieces with its knife. It was a distant wailing, like a sad animal whose beauty was being strangled away. So sad it was, so achingly haunting, that the little mermaid began to follow it, forgetting there was ever a God at all.

The music, for it was indeed music that she heard, led her around the beach, where it abruptly ended in majestic limestone cliffs. The cliffs seemed to ascend to the stars, and as she swam around the coastline, she was accosted by an amazing sight.

A palace, of the kind the little mermaid could only dream of, seemed to materialise out of the limestone cliffs, trickle down to the shore and plunge into the ocean. A gorgeous, decadent structure of stone and glass, its towers and upper halls were indeed carved out of the enormous cliffs, where it evolved into balconies and terraces of stone. As she peered closely, she could distinguish courtyards and clock towers beyond the balconies, and gardens whose fragrance punctured the breeze. But perhaps the most remarkable of all its features was the way the palace poured onto the ocean, the reflection of the moon shimmering in the glassy walls and tiles. There were paths across the water's surface that led from chamber to chamber, and open hallways lit by dozens of lanterns, so unobstructed that you or I could swim between the corridors of royalty. Her father's palace, in all of its splendour, seemed cheap and false in comparison.

The music lured her to approaching the palace, and the mermaid soon found herself amongst the very same passages that lay unfenced on the calm, shallow waters. Dazzled as she was, she failed to notice that the music had stopped. Instead she busied herself peering into the large glass windows of each passing chamber. She loved the chandeliers affixed to the ceilings that warmed the room with a golden glow. The little tongues of red wind that danced atop candlesticks transfixed her. She inhaled the coats of arms and patriotic flags, royal emblems and tapestries. Even the furnishings and carpets nourished her, and she mistook a harpsichord for a magnificent sleeping beast. She nourished her soul on each and every item until all of the lower chambers, the sea-level subsection of the palace, had been discovered.

An alarm began to sound in the mermaid's mind as the Finfolk's spell began to wear off. As she prepared to leave, she noticed the same red wind dancing in a darkened room beyond, at the very end of the passage. She approached, and through a silver-paned window, she saw a man.

He was lying on a large, canopied bed in the middle of a vast room. It would have boasted the most hedonistic of worldly goods, had it not been cloaked in darkness. In fact, the only light in the room was from a single candle, burning carelessly from where it was lodged into the cover of a book, thrown to the floor in a fit of boredom. Puddles of wax hardened beneath it. The mermaid shuddered, and every pore of her skin drunk him in, for this was the first human she had ever laid eyes on. She devoured him with her gaze.

He was unlike anything she had imagined. She had surmised that human beings were merely merfolk with legs, for that was the way her sisters had described them. And what legs they were! But they were covered, as was his whole body, with thick and flowing cloth that seemed to mould to every angle. The little mermaid was instantly ashamed of her nakedness, and folded her arms over her bare breast. As she peered closer, she realised that he was no man but a boy, with his hands behind his head, and a leg swinging absently from the bed, childishly. She created parallels in her mind: for he was a prince and she was a princess, and they were similar in age, and in a single moment she could see an entire lifetime of parallels between them.

It was his face that entranced her the most. It was so beautiful that it was sure to sell for enormous amounts if she peeled it from his skull. She especially liked the black curls that fell on his forehead. She didn't know hair could fall like that. He had elegant brown hands with long shapely fingers, and as they escaped the tangle of his curls, the little mermaid imagined his palms pressing into the nape of her neck. But then she recalled her own unsightly gills, heaving heavily now from rejecting the air, red, seething, ugly gashes. How they would surely repel a man like him.

It did not yet seem unnatural to her as the Prince drew a dagger from his side, and it winked in the candlelight. It did not interrupt the eerie allure of the scene as the boy slowly stroked his throat with its gleaming narrow blade. He held it up to the window, examining it, his eyes barely skirting the top of the mermaid's head as she ducked, blood pounding in her ears. When she summoned enough courage to raise herself back to the window, she saw that he had rolled onto his stomach, sighing deeply, the dagger gone. There was a little glint on his face, like water caught in the light.

He was alarmed by a sudden pounding at the door. The little mermaid, in a state of panic yet strangely elated, returned to the depths, the spell all but faded away.

Before the Prince could stash the dagger deeper inside the snarl of sheets, the door opened and the room was flooded with light. He shielded his eyes and opened his mouth to reprimand the visitor when he heard an old voice, a much-loved voice call his name.

The boy scrambled to his feet and hurried to the man. "Uncle," he said, and allowed himself to be drawn into long-awaited arms like a child. "The advisors told me they could not find you."

"It isn't their fault," said the man. "I can't be found if I don't wish to be. I came as soon as I heard."

The young Prince looked up at the careworn face before him, a face smeared with sun and wind, sweat and heartbreak. He smelled like he hadn't washed in weeks. His hair grew over his collar, and a heavy beard concealed a face that was caught in the middle years. But the Prince didn't care. "Where were you?" he asked, and his voice was high-pitched, if not a little shaky.

"Romania," replied his Uncle nonchalantly, shrugging.

"Where's that?"

The Uncle eyed his nephew carefully. "It's one country of many that you must not only learn of, but maintain peace with, now that you are King."

"King!" spat the boy, and he turned his back on his Uncle and moved to the window, gazing out to sea.

The Uncle examined the chamber with disapproval. "And now that you are King, these rooms will not do. They are too easily penetrated, any assassin could creep here in the middle of the night and take your life."

"My guards are right outside the door."

"Your guards are so dense they will think twice if they hear you scream."

"I prefer them that way," said the boy, with the air of someone who spends a great deal of time screaming. "And I don't care if some assassin wants to kill me. They'd be doing the kingdom a favour."

"Don't talk rot," snapped the Uncle.

"And what about you?" sneered the boy. "You're the real King, the Prince *Regent*. Isn't that why you really came back? My father is dead, and haven't you always wanted his throne?"

He was not insulted by the boy's wild accusations, instead he was sorry for this young life already affected so painfully by tragedy. The Prince's words were true, as the King's brother he could readily take the throne. But as a man who enjoyed the rank and privileges connected with sovereignty, he did not relish the responsibility, and had never hankered for more power than he already had. "You are of age now, my boy. You are neither too young nor incapacitated. There is no court in the land that would grant me ruling."

The boy's eyes were wild with fever. "But I'll give you the kingdom," he gushed. "Don't you understand? It's yours. I don't want it."

"With your every word, your infantile experience becomes more apparent. What makes you think I'd ever come back here? Don't you remember what happened?"

The Prince understood, but he was not prepared to listen. "Oh, *that*. That was ages ago, Uncle. Surely you are passed all that? All of your gallivanting around the continent, the world no less? Oh, you ran so far. You ran to Antarctica! Or did you think I was too *infantile* to know where that was?"

But the Uncle was too wise and too kind to rise to the bait. "I only returned because my dear brother has died, and his own son needs me."

The Prince's face crumpled as if he might cry, but he steeled himself. I cannot do this," he admitted. "I was not born to be a King. I want to go away, far away. I want to be like you." His eyes brightened with an unnatural light. "Let's leave," he said, "and just disappear. And the whole world will think we are dead, and go on without us."

But his Uncle shook his head. "And leave all the good work your father did undone?"

A sliver of guilt plucked at the Prince now, for he remembered his father, and the hardships he had endured. He recalled the atmosphere of the whole world on the day he was born. The tension, like a dry bone with no marrow, aching to snap. The evacuations, the invasions. Waking up to the view of a thousand bodies decapitated on the shores of this very coast. Marching in the funeral procession of his own mother, in trousers too long that nobody had thought to hem.

He watched agony and strain age his father beyond recognition. He endured the long absences, months spent with his gut so twisted that doctors foretold his own death if he did not soon defecate, all because he was never sure that his father would return. But the King won the alliance of all the neighbouring kingdoms one by one, and once he had achieved peace in all the land, he returned to the palace and never left again. In fact, he promptly died of exhaustion, leaving a son he barely knew, but a kingdom ripe on the cusp of greatness.

"I will undo every good thing he ever did. I know nothing about running a kingdom."

"You will learn."

"He taught me nothing!"

"His lords and advisors are worthy men, and they will—"

"Those old fools? It was my father who did the real work, and they just went around collecting taxes and glory!" The Prince began to pace around the room darkly. "No, no, they will conspire against me. They want the kingdom for themselves!"

"Forgive me, my lad, but it seems to me that the only thing standing between you and your kingdom is the very great likeness you have to a menstruating woman."

The Prince stopped still like he was punched in the

jaw. He turned to his uncle, eyes wide with astonishment. "What did you say?" he stammered.

"I said you're like a woman," was the calm reply.

"A *woman?*"

"A woman!" roared his Uncle. "A woman on her menses, crying one moment, looking for a fight the next! Driving mad all the men in her household! But on second thoughts, to compare you to a woman seems an insult to the worthy sex. No, you're a wilful, disobedient puppy who doesn't respect his master and discharges filth all over the house, despite his training. You're irrational and weak and ridiculous! Where's your backbone? Where is your courage? I thought my brother died and left a son, the very image of himself. But I am convinced you don't have a single drop of his blood in your veins."

Enraged, the Prince flung himself to his bed to retrieve the dagger from within the sheets. "You bastard!" he screamed, "Who invited you here? Who sent for you?" In a wild temper, the Prince flung the dagger at his Uncle, but his Uncle was gone. Instead, the dagger shivered, embedded in the closed door. The candle had gone out.

"A woman," he said to the darkness. "I am no woman."

FIVE

AMIDST THE PARALLELS

THE WHOLE WORLD was swimming. The little mermaid was experiencing a sort of vertigo, where nothing that was still stayed that way, and the things that ought to move froze stiff. Her entire life felt topsy-turvy, and though she had but a small taste of the land above the surface, now she craved more. When she had returned to the palace, where her sisters and nanny awaited her dutifully, it was more of a struggle than ever to keep her face straight and her voice from wavering frequency to frequency. She reported all she had seen, and could not stop her eyes lighting up when she described the remarkable palace on the shore.

"The human palace?" asked the eldest. "But it is ordinary. It is nothing like our home."

"Why do you praise it so? It is so ugly, like it was built by blind men," remarked the second eldest.

The youngest princess was astonished by her sisters' response and more than a little disheartened, for she was sure that they would be in agreement – wouldn't anyone who had seen it concur it was miraculous? So she turned her attention to something she was sure would be a success.

"What about the Prince who lives there? Surely he is beautiful."

"If he were one of us, perhaps."

"It's a shame about those human legs. Unpleasant, graceless things."

"He is only beautiful when he sleeps."

"But his skin is so dark, like the colour of dirt."

"And his eyes so plain."

"And he makes the most horrendous noises."

"Dreadful hollering and wailing all night long."

"It hurts our ears to hear it."

"It is the most inhumane noise." The little mermaid knew they were referring to the music, and how often it omitted from the Prince. The thought filled her with thick pleasure for the music too, just like everything about him, was more attractive than seemed possible.

"Is something the matter, sister?" asked the sixth princess, the closest to her in age and therefore the dearest. For the little mermaid was wearing a vacant expression and in her mind's eye was a small collection of images she had carefully memorised about him. There was almost as much pleasure in imagining the unknown: the Prince eating, for instance, or the sound of his voice, or what he looked like under his clothes. The nanny eyed her cautiously, for she had seen that expression before, although she did not remember where.

She could not sleep that night, instead she relived every detail of her visit, the smells and the sounds she heard. The sensation of the waves as they curled around her body. The taste of sea foam – the ashes of her kin. She formed a secret plan to visit again the next night, for as the only princess to exhibit the quality of curiosity, she had searched every nook and cranny of her palace, and knew where everything was stored. Like the pieces of shattered looking-glass, so old and forgotten barnacles had settled upon them. And remnants of hair, long black strands littered with sea-lice, accompanied by a whole fingernail, all prudently wrapped in sea-weed and stored in an empty crevice. She knew precisely where the potion was stored, and though it was easy to simply ask her father for protection to surface, she did not want to answer questions.

Indeed, this was strange, because all of her life the little mermaid had longed for questions. She simply did not understand why she was not often asked where she was going or who with. Often she went to dangerous places and saw dangerous things, and if anyone could prevent her, it should be a parent. And nobody ever asked her how she felt inside, especially at that moment when she was about to explode with something and desperately wanted to be asked about it, in order to diffuse her emotion or to delay it. But it never came. The little mermaid concluded it had a lot to do with her sisters, who never went anywhere except the well-lit courtyards of the palace and its domain, and never saw anyone more than their own reflections. She used to prattle in her younger years, unable to hold in the rush of thoughts, but it pained the nanny, or anyone else who heard her. So she kept most things to herself, picturing her insides like a treasure trove, and would turn over these thoughts softly in her hands, like well-loved toys. But this time it was different. She was aware that to answer questions about her immediate surfacing could be fatal, and she was resolved to one more secret.

The next night, anticipation flooded her as she ventured toward the palace, which beckoned to her seductively and winked with its warm, flickering candlelight. Exotic spices were in the air and the little mermaid rubbed her gooseflesh impatiently. She did not bother to examine the other chambers, swimming directly to the Prince's, only to find he was not inside. Filled with hope, she settled herself comfortably, folding and tucking her fins behind her, and waited. But he did not come. When the potion began to wear away, the mermaid sighed deeply and her heart sank into her stomach.

She returned the next night, praying to see the little red wind dancing in his window, but the chamber was buried in darkness. Had she imagined him? Did he now sleep in the upper levels? Perhaps he had spotted her and was frightened, requesting to be as far away from her as possible. Perhaps, and the mermaid shuddered at the thought, he had died, and his dear Immortal Soul had gone to God. In which case, the mermaid was glad for him, but hopelessly miserable for herself. Suddenly, the music started. Far above her it lilted, deep and wounded and dripping all over her like syrup. She craned her neck to catch a glimpse of him, high in the terraces or even the mountaintop, but she saw nothing. But she was consoled, for she felt his presence, and understood the music was for her.

On the third night, the little mermaid was preparing to leave when her nanny approached her.

"Are you going up to the human palace again?" she asked.

"Yes," the little mermaid replied.

"Are you going to see the Prince?"

"I am," she said, for she could not tell a lie.

"Then see him, observe him, but hide yourself well. For he will sooner slit your throat and devour you than speak to you."

"I don't think that he would –"

"This is not the way to gain an Immortal Soul, my dear," said the nanny gently.

The little mermaid halted. "I know, nanny, of course it isn't."

"For a human man has to hold you in higher regard than even his own father," she continued, "and commit to you in the ceremony of marriage. Then a piece of his soul will enter your body, and one day you too will be with God."

The little mermaid shivered, for it was the happiest news she'd ever heard. "Truly?" she asked.

"Of course," replied the nanny.

It wasn't. Many years ago, some merfolk had started the rumour partly due to boredom, for there was not a vast amount of things to do in the underwater world, apart from gander at pretty things, and lose a pretty thing to gain another pretty thing. But the nanny did not know this and neither did our impressionable heroine. And she believed it with her whole heart.

"But it is not possible, for human beings are not inclined toward our kind," said the nanny finally, and the mermaid pressed her hands against her ugly gills and tried not to believe it.

"Caution, my dear," warned the nanny, "you are crossing a fine line. Do you really wish to die of heartbreak?"

"But nanny," whispered the little mermaid, edging closer and forgetting to conceal her curiosity, "what causes heartbreak?"

A cloud passed over the nanny's features and she dropped her gaze. It was a long time before she spoke again, as she battled against her own better judgement. After what seemed an eternity, she opened her eyes and said quietly, "It is something we merfolk are forbidden to mention. It is something that was outlawed a long time ago, something that we have since forgotten."

The little mermaid's eyes shone with feverish excitement. "But *you* haven't forgotten," she prompted.

"Alas, my dear," sighed the nanny. "I never knew it in the first place. But I am sure it is something terrible, for it fractures the human's living hearts so permanently that they die. Imagine then what it would do to the empty hearts of we merfolk. For us, it would be worse than death."

So when the little mermaid returned to shore again, her mind was full of imaginings and further parallels were created between herself and the Prince. She considered the ceremony of marriage and what it would feel like to have a part of the Prince's Immortal Soul breathing inside of her.

She also pondered the Great Condition, and what it could do to her own dead heart. These thoughts kept her warm as she waited patiently outside his dark window, and for a few radiant moments, she heard his song in the high wings of the palace.

Once she heard the scraping of a boot on the stone above her, and spray of pebble showered her as she ducked underwater for cover. She looked up through the water and thought she saw a creature so white it was transparent, with milky eyes staring down at her malevolently. But when she drew closer, she found it was nothing but the moon.

The King's brother was worried for the boy. After their altercation earlier in the week, the Prince continued to be sullen and moody. He kept to himself and would regularly practice avoiding the court and advisors. The Uncle had tried to apologise for his fit of temper but the boy would not hear of it. He behaved as if everyone he encountered were a spy or an enemy. He disappeared from sight frequently during the day and was so evasive that his Uncle was forced to all but drag him from his bedchamber in the evenings to attend to official business.

Although he was never a happy child, his Uncle had to admit that he had altered significantly during his absence, for the Prince was deeply morose and was adamant that he did not want the throne. The lords and councillors took to meeting privately to discuss the idea of replacement, and distant relatives had been found as far away as Brussels. These relations were sure to be salivating with ambition, but the Uncle rued the day his brother's kingdom would fall into a stranger's hands. He would rather take the throne himself.

And so he did, non-officially, tying up the loose ends left by the King, and unravelling the tangles that his nephew was too young to understand. He spent his free hours mourning. As he walked the corridors he was interrupted by many ghosts, and sometimes they took him away for a spell to recall a happy memory spent together in this very palace.

The Prince meanwhile, roamed the palace also, but aimlessly, his expression so dark that the ghosts were frightened to approach him. He immersed himself in the grand library, searching through books, throwing them aside when useless or ripping away their pages when frustrated. He would dodge the advisors, resorting to darting behind statues or clambering up trees, in an undignified non-Prince-like fashion.

Sometimes he would enter the King's bedchamber, the curtains drawn against the musty scent. He would creep across the foot of the stately bed on his hands and knees and curl into a cannonball, dense and impenetrable. Occasionally he would fall asleep. Other times, he would imagine himself taking residency in these rooms. Then he would strip off his clothes and stand in front of his father's looking-glass, and his eyes would search out the well-known imperfections of his body, and he would curse himself and his ugliness. Sometimes he would put on his father's cloak, and the plush velvet would brush against his shoulders and buttocks, and he would muse how unlike his father he was, how weak and sickly in comparison. And then his dog, the little black creature he had adopted as a child, would growl low in her throat and they would leave.

He had found the pup along the beach, a bedraggled puny thing, washed up from the wreck of some merchant ship or another. Like any boy, he was delighted with the prospect of a docile companion, albeit soon burdened with its care and constant companionship. For the dog was like a shadow, and the Prince would often trip over it, or the tiresome thing would wail and whimper if the Prince attended to other things. On an especially frustrating day, of which his tutors had turned in a unsatisfactory report, his father reprimanding him heartily, the Prince returned to his chamber to find his dog excitable, barking and jumping and running its claws over his breeches. So tired and despondent was he that every infernal sound that came from the dog's mouth was like knitting needles driven into his brain. The claws were like fingernails dragged over his skin and the sheer deliriousness of his pet reminded him of his incapacity of even making a dog happy. So he beat her. The dog had scampered from him, bleating a sorrowful little wail. Ridden with guilt, the Prince crept up to where she was shivering in a corner, reaching out to stroke her head. But the dog cowered, and a blind rage overcame the Prince. How dare she misread him! How dare she be frightened of the only one that loved her! So he beat her again, and louder grew her cries, until he forgot who he was and who she was, and his boot found her tender side. The dog howled and disappeared.

Before you judge the Prince, look back on your own life. Are you so blameless that you would turn against him now, in his greatest need? Have you not yourself committed disgraceful acts, let the streak of cruelty inherent in human nature possess you for a moment? Then there is that scenario you've blotted out of your memory, or excused because you were young, and it was a phase. Well, the Prince is young, and it is a phase. And if you knew him better, you would not run to the shore to warn the mermaid away. You would wait and see.

There were several reasons why the Prince chosen to house himself sea-level. Firstly, it guaranteed solitude, as prominent members of the court preferred their lodgings higher in the terraces. They liked to rise with the sun in their windows, dress and receive a bountiful breakfast brought by the palace maids. They preferred to roam about the atriums and sunlit halls with their colleagues and discuss the latest events, even venture to the gardens to look at the ladies. They would drink tea with lemon, awaiting summons to this meeting or that council from the King's brother, all pretending they did not see the Prince where he was perched in a tree. No one at all resided in the sea chambers except the Prince, for that level had been primarily intended for music and entertainment, and to show off the great talent of the architect, all of which the palace had seen little lately. So the Prince would mope and lament and curse and make all manner of ungodly noises undetected, and everyone was happy until his damned uncle had to show up and make a mess of things.

Secondly, the Prince understood that being sea-level was the closest he was going to get to being separated from the world, for now. He hated everyone. His advisors were like candy to him, tasting good but eventually rotting the teeth. The women were ridiculous, he hated the way their skirts twirled around them when they danced, making them appear like spinning marshmallows. He hated their simpering voices and the sound of giggling, and he particularly loathed it when they would push each other forward to talk to him, and then insist on discussing inane topics he had no interest in. He found womenfolk a huge waste of time and space, and felt that the council would be much more productive if they were not present. If he ever took up the kingship, he was determined to rid the court of them as soon as possible. At the back of his mind, it lingered that he would one day be required to take a wife himself, but had decided to postpone it until his elderly years, when he was too old to sire children, for a child of his was sure to be a child cursed. For his abject behaviour toward women, he was aware that there were some reports circulating about him, some of which were unpleasant to dwell upon. For example, after a particular occasion where a wealthy and powerful woman had tried unsuccessfully to seduce him, she had hissed a word, just one word, under her breath before she stalked away. The word, which shall not be mentioned here, could only mean a single thing: *man-lover*. But the Prince did not understand, for he hated everyone, man and woman alike, and the only thing that made men slightly more preferable in his sight was the fact that he belonged to the gender, and understood them more.

Thirdly, the Prince had heard a rumour many years earlier, and these days found that it utterly consumed him. It was said that beyond the land and beyond the ocean lay a strange world, a world caught inside the very core of the earth, a place where time did not exist. There were creatures there, spirits, if you will, that would grant you one wish. He had heard reports that such wishes were varied and extreme: the sultan of Arabia had once been a beggar who had sought the spirits, and a woman who had wanted many children but only wished to bear the pain but one time, birthed quintuplets, a phenomenon unheard of in the day. Limbs had been restored, lives prolonged beyond what seemed respectable, kingdoms torn apart and rebuilt, new stars added to the sky. The spirits had been granting wishes for thousands of years, although nobody had ever met a successful recipient of such wishes, it was all through friends-of-friends, or stories passed along by weary travellers.

All the reports agreed that the journey there was perilous. It was no simple matter to pass all land and water, and nobody knew how to go or where to start. The exact location of the spirits was a mystery, some said they lived in the deepest part of the ocean, others that they moved position with every new moon. There was debate as to the methodology of the whole business: some said you fell into a coma and awoke in the core of earth, others that you drowned and woke up a spirit too, enabling you to communicate with the others. Alternative gossip said that it was all a costly illusion: for to behold these beings you must surely die, and the spirits were the angels of God, and you were doomed to roam the earth a ghost, believing your wishes to have been granted, all a sordid punishment for the unforgivable sin of suicide.

The Prince had taken all of these bits of information and held them to his heart, stroking them with every ounce of affection he gave to his dog. He turned them over and over in his mind, like uncooked pancakes. He dreamed about the beings. In his wildest fantasies they granted him his one wish, and all the world was righted and he felt that burning in his chest, the burning he had not felt in years: happiness. He searched the great literary works of the known world for hints, indications of where they might lie. He read about the lives of extraordinary people in history, wondering if the spirits had influenced the chronology of events. He felt that he should try, and was perfectly content to die trying, for death would be preferable to the stagnant life he led. In truth, he longed for death, although he was too frightened to do the act himself.

When he was required to attend church, he would kneel before the sacrament and pray that God bestow upon him a disease, or to let him die in his sleep. When this did not avail, he would curse God, heaving obscenities toward his son Jesu, in hopes that he would strike him with lightening. As the Prince grew older, he stopped believing in God, and took to carving little straight lines into himself with his dagger, watching in wonder as the blood formed on his skin in tiny crimson droplets, which he sometimes tasted but mainly wiped away. His arms and thighs bore the evidence of these acts performed by candlelight, raised lattice-work of where, after years of self-mutilation, scars had formed over scars, disappointment over disappointment.

Finally, the time came when the Prince was prepared to let go. The plans he had been consciously forming for years were ready to be utilised, beginning with the boat he had docked past the water passages and the staircase that led to the sea, moored to the furthest pier. He took nothing but his courage, and as he ventured along the passages toward the boat, even the moon hid its face in fright. The Prince grasped the oars. He cut the rope.

SIX

DROWN

THE LITTLE MERMAID was more than disheartened, for weeks had passed without a single, solitary
glimpse of the Prince. In fact, she had seen no one and would
have believed it all an illusion had it not been for the glorious music that sometimes would float down the tiers of the
palace. She had the sensation of being watched, but it was a
pleasant and comforting feeling, rather than sinister.

If merfolk were blessed with intuition, her sisters would
have asked what was wrong with her, for when she returned
to the underwater palace in the early hours, she was utterly
spent, and when she emerged from her long, fitful sleeps, she
looked a wraith herself. It was partly due to the nightmares.
She had had the same dream since she first saw the Prince,
of which she was constantly running. All was in darkness,
and she was being chased by an albino spectre, whose limbs

were skeletal and scaly, its only distinguishing feature being a patch on its back that sprouted thick, wiry hairs.

But the little mermaid's long vigil was rewarded when one night, as she waited by the Prince's window, a candle was lit. Gleefully, she peered into the darkness and as the familiar canopied bed and rich furnishings became apparent, a living creature within her chest suddenly leapt forward, threatening to escape her throat. For there was the Prince, and he was more beautiful than she remembered. Her breathing ceased and the creature pounded within her so hard that it hurt. She painfully watched his movements, which were slow and precise, as he gathered meagre belongings and draped himself in a long cloak the colour of night. He blew out the candle and all was darkness.

The princess was disconcerted, for she had waited long and hard for this moment, and the moment had passed too soon. However, she soon became alert to the sound of footsteps, loud against her ears, yet quickly fading away. As silently as she could, she followed them toward the ocean, occasionally lifting her head from the water to gauge direction. And then she saw him, sliding into a small rowboat. The dagger glinted as he cut it free.

Filled with joy, the mermaid swam alongside him, close enough to escort the boat, but deep enough that she remained invisible. Sometimes she grew tired and grasped the hull of the boat, letting it bear her through strong currents. She cautiously avoided the oars as they dipped into the water, but even if she were careless, the Prince was too occupied to notice.

It was a moonless night, and soon the little mermaid became disoriented, and lost her bearings. The boat stopped in the cold, pre-dawn hours and the mermaid waited, shivering. An anchor dropped beside her, the rope unravelling until it could unravel no more - futile really, for the ocean was too deep. Still, she coiled her tail around it for support, for she was growing weary. Her eyes were fixed on the surface, and she waited.

Suddenly, something plunged into the ocean and began to sink. Frightened, the little mermaid froze, unwilling to move and alert a potential predator. But the dark mass did not acknowledge her, and continued its descent, occasionally struggling and writhing in the water. Gingerly, the little mermaid approached it. As she began to realise what it was, fascination overcame her, for surely it was her Prince! She was filled with joy, for she was undoubtedly the reason for all this! He had noticed her outside his window all along, and wooed her with his song, and upon discovery of what she was, had made arrangements to be with her! But her victorious elation soon gave way to a gnawing horror as she noticed that his hands and feet were clumsily bound together, as if self-done, and that he had attempted to wind and knot the cloak over himself, like gift-wrap. And the wise words of her nanny came back to her, "They drown because they cannot breath the water."

Hastily, she grabbed at the Prince and shook him. His eyes did not open, and his head fell so far back that she could see the beautiful gobbet of his throat. Struggling with all her might, she grasped at the cloak and began to drag him toward the surface. But all she succeeded in doing was unravelling it, and the Prince plummeted further into the depths. Panicked, she chased after him and finally managed to insert her head into the crook of his underarm. Pushing against his elbow and waist, she used every ounce of might to propel him upward, wondering in the back of her mind how long humans could survive without air.

Finally, she pushed him through the last barrier and positioned him on his back upon the water's surface, holding his head in her hands and willing him to breathe. He did not. She shook him, bewildered, unwilling to let go. She craned her head to find the boat but the sea was covered with a thick fog. It was impossible. Eventually, her head bent close over his, she detected his shallow, minute breathing.

Slowly, she began to drag the Prince away, for she was aware he was freezing, his fingers were icy and still. She did not know where land was, and was unfamiliar with the path of the sun, so she lugged his body with her remaining energy to wherever she reckoned land may be. She tried to calm herself, to still the thumping creature inside her, and tried to ignore the questions – what was he trying to do? *Was he trying to die?* On and on she hauled the Prince, stopping every now and then to check his breathing, which was ragged and shallow. She heard the cries of the flying fish and was encouraged, and all around her the seas turned to a pale gold and she realised dawn was coming.

Through the mist, she saw a tower and inside that tower was a bell. With aching arms she heaved him onto the beach, and collapsed beside him.

The sound of chimes awoke her and hastily she hoisted herself upright, bending her head toward the Prince's, satisfied to hear his strong, regular breathing. There was something else too, the sound of beating, a very dull and muffled sound that filled the space between them. Alert now, with the God climbing higher in the sky, she fumbled with the ropes tied crudely around the boy's limbs, and after much ado completed freeing his wrists and ankles. Sighing with relief, she gazed down at him and was contented to see the glow had returned to his cheek and the warmth to his forehead. She reached out a hand, very tentatively, and ran it lightly over his face, so delicately it was certain he could not feel it. But he opened his eyes.

He was dazed and confused and his first thought was that she did not look at all how he had imagined the beings, and he opened his mouth to say so. But at that moment, the peal of bells overcame him, as did the sound of many footsteps, and there were cries overhead and a great deal of splashing. Slipping back into unconciousness, he did not see the stream of uniformed girls surround him, screaming and gaggling so furiously that two formidable nuns were required to subdue them. Some of the girls they managed to order back to their dormitories, and some slipped away out of a sense of duty to the morning mass, but one in particular stayed behind and watched solemnly as the Mother Superior herself pumped the boy's chest and laid her head against it for a heart beat.

It was this girl, this very neat and tidy and ordinary girl, that the Prince remembered for years to come, when he was no longer prince but king of all the land, and one of the greatest kings that the realm would ever know. He would eventually lean against the armrest of his throne and recall the way she stood so still, her hands perfectly folded inside the other. The way her great eyes absorbed him without so much as blinking, and especially the way she seemed so small, so inconsequential, at the convent where the oranges grew.

WHAT LIES IN THE BLOODSTREAM

THERE WAS SOMETHING dreadfully wrong. The little mermaid could feel it in her every blood cell, in every gulp of water inhaled and filtered by those infernal gills. Nothing tasted the same and the food certainly would not stay put in her stomach. All day long her innards churned, and her mind raced, and her soul longed. And the creature inside her chest, lodged between her ribcage, would beat so hard that she was sure her sisters would hear – and that would be a very bad thing, she decided. She had a creeping, guilty feeling it. She knew what had awakened it and that it was unnatural.

She had returned to the palace, night after night, and still there was no sign of the Prince. But the little mermaid was no fool, for she knew she had left him alive and eventually he would return. A liquid giddiness would fill her bloodstream when she thought his name and sometimes she whispered it in the dark. It was enough to chill her, and send her flying backwards through wild imaginings and scenes and daydreams, where she watched more than his Immortal Soul wind around her and breathe into her ear. She had memorised every contour of his face. Her fingers still tingled in memory of his skin. It was something dreadfully right.

She felt she would burst, and she had to tell someone. The little mermaid isolated the sixth princess one day and said, "Sister, what do you know of the sea-witch?"

The second youngest princess blinked her large, empty eyes and recited, "She is an evil woman who lives beyond the gorge. She is a collector of body parts and other horrible things. They say she drinks her own blood."

"But she makes spells?"

"Yes, yes, but spells for the outcasts, potions for unnatural requests."

The little mermaid was growing excited. "Unnatural? Like transformation? Or metamorphosis?"

"Yes, I suppose so. "

"Or an Immortal Soul?"

"Perhaps, but nobody wants one of those." Her sister was tiring of the conversation, as it did not revolve around food, beauty or herself.

"Sister," said the little mermaid, lowering her voice, "do you know how to get there?"

"You will have to ask Father."

"I want to keep it a secret. You understand, don't you?"

The very old inbuilt alarm began to sound somewhere

within her sister, the siren that was always intended for use but instead, lay deep inside each mer-person, covered in cobwebs. "Don't go," she said, her voice deepening, "Not even Father would go there. Don't go."

"But I must," said the little mermaid, for it seemed the only way.

"Why?" asked her sister.

"Because," stated the little mermaid mournfully, "I am in love."

As soon as the word left her lips, it hung there, suspended in the water for an eternity. She had never heard the word before but there it was, spelled out in front of her in all its weight and consequence, and she understood its body and its bones. Her sister stared at it, and a light that wasn't there before suddenly flared in her eye like a beacon. She inhaled the word. She tried to resist it, but it entered her bloodstream.

"Don't go," repeated her sister, and the luminescence in her eyes frightened the little mermaid.

"Don't tell anyone!" hissed the little mermaid.

The plan had been brewing in the mermaid's mind for weeks. She believed that the idea first occurred to her when she left the Prince on the shore and returned to her home. It was her very good fortune that she was not attacked by gypsies on her way, for she had spent a great deal of time being lost, as she was weary and dazed. But even without the potion, she had never shone quite as brightly as her sisters, and had not attracted as much attention as they. When schools of commoners passed, she concealed herself behind the banks of the reeds, and nobody was the wiser. However, the notion did not occur there, where she watched the everyday people go about their rituals, but when she was suspended beneath the boat, waiting for something to happen. When the Prince was mere meters away, tying the ropes around his own wrists, and the only sound to be heard was the beating in her chest.

Throughout the past few weeks, she had felt the Prince gradually begin to take hold of her. It had not started small, like most raging addictions, with a reckless decision or two steps in the wrong direction. From the first time she saw him, he took a hold of all the scapes of her imagination. But ever since she had seen him descending into darkness, he possessed the creature that lived inside her, the noisy and unfamiliar thing that whispered in a voice of its own. As soon as she felt the creature awake, she knew that her whole life was over and she had to recover a new one, one that would ensure her nearness to the Prince, one that would see the parallels become reality.

Her need overcame her fear of the witch's reputation, and the creature inside her was not to be ignored, for it had whispered the plan to her in the dark. The deciding factor had been the potion. She had used the entire stock of the very expensive protective tonic that her Father had negotiated for, and she knew she had no chance of returning to the surface unharmed without it. But the notion of visiting the Finfolk abhorred her, although she knew the way. It had little to do with the Finfolk themselves, none of which the princess had ever seen, but the gorge and what lay beneath. Just thinking of the gorge struck her with paralysing fear, and she knew that the creatures that lay beyond it were not her friends, but her enemy. So she swallowed the very last drops of the potion, and in the dead of the dark where her father and sisters and all that she knew slept soundly, she disappeared in search of the witch.

She did not know in which direction lay the witch's lair, but instinct told her to follow the commoner's trail. So she did, swimming the opposite way to where her and her sisters would regularly frequent, away from the shining gold reefs, and the great oyster fields that harvested the royal pearls. She passed over the homes of the commoners, ordinary structures made of practical stone, most of which without as much as a shell embellishment, for shells were expensive as they were found, with great peril, on the shore. There were fewer orbs here, as the poor did not have as much right to the light as the rich (and had less pretty things to look at, so none was wasted) and the little mermaid found that a very great comfort, as the orbs had always unnerved her.

A few miles of this led to a sort of wasteland, a shallow and arid place where the soil was grey and barren, as plants and animals had been strangled to death by the crown-of-thorns that ravaged the landscape. On the banks of the wastelands lay the graveyard, miles and miles of wreckage and rock, heaved there by raw brawn from all over the ocean. Grand, sunken vestiges of magnificent ships, little scrappy rowboats, huge steel cargo vessels were all home to the gypsy folk, who sold their bodies for food. It was little wonder, for there were no living creatures to eat in this part of the ocean, save for barnacles and the odd clam. The sea-gypsies often sent out their whollest and strongest to hunt the larger predators, but these were becoming rarer as they avoided the merfolk kingdom. But still, they preferred the wastelands to the centre of the kingdom, where they were shunned and mistreated. Many a merchant would raise their prices when the gypsies came to buy, for no one wanted to consort with them. Even their dead fish were too good for them.

When the ships began to fall apart, the water-worms corroding the wood, the gypsies would depart for search of another home. They were a stubborn people and they stayed together, a menagerie of inter-related families, and often twenty or thirty of them would live together, all on top of the other in a single vessel, and nobody complained. The little mermaid sucked in her breath and swam a good distance over them, and hoped to remain undetected.

After a long time, the little mermaid was swimming in water so dark that she could not see her hands in front of her face. She was entertaining thoughts of turning back and trying another way, when out of the blackness, three very white creatures appeared. They hovered in the water and stared at her, and the little mermaid recognised them although they looked quite different from how they usually appeared. They began to sing:

> *"Turn away, child of the land*
> *Far from the breast you came*
> *Returning now into the hand*
> *That sewed you inside pain*
> *For in this world, what you seek*
> *Has died yet lies beyond*
> *Your blood will pour, your screams ignored*
> *In the place where you came from."*

Now the little mermaid was not like the others who had heard the Siren's song before her, for she had heard music and she had heard voices other than her species, and she distinguished the words clearly. She turned them over in her mind as she followed the Sirens to their destination, and tried to memorise them, in case they were important later.

They passed over the garden where the plants had faces, and little voices reached the mermaid's ears. "Help us," they cried mostly, and "turn back". But the mermaid was determined and so she ignored them. As they approached the cavern with its cloak of menace thrown over it, the little mermaid steeled herself and thought of the Prince. She entered the cave, and immediately felt at ease, for the room was bathed in the light of the torch-fish, so impenetrable and dim.

A terrible sound began to fill the room. It echoed in every corner and grew louder and louder. The Sirens clutched each other and retreated. The little mermaid was ashamed to cause such alarm, for she was sure the pounding was her own. But it wasn't.

When the sea-witch entered the cavern, the little mermaid did not have the experience that so many others before her did, of déjà vu and vertigo. In fact, the sea-witch did not have any affect on her at all, because she had never seen her before in her life. Where other folk would become confounded and recall the witch's face from the earliest moments of their lives, the princess saw nothing and felt nothing. But the sea-witch affixed a keen eye on her, and approached her cautiously, her monstrous black tail writhing beneath her, and her hair billowing dark and lustrous.

"Ah," she said, "it *is* you. I wasn't sure I would recall, but I see *him* in you."

The little mermaid, who had heard reports that the sea-witch greatly enjoyed clouding her victim's minds with strange words and riddles, said plainly, "I wish to be made a human."

But the witch did not respond. She stretched out a white hand toward the little mermaid's face, her expression fathomless. For a wild moment, the mermaid thought she meant to claw at her face with aged talons. But after a second, the witch grimaced and rapidly pulled her hand away.

"A human," she repeated in flat tones. "Why would anyone want to become that?"

"Because I love a human," replied the little mermaid, "and I wish to be with him always."

"Love?" hissed the sea-witch, recoiling. "What is *love*?" And she turned her back on her guest to face the wall. After a while, she whirled around and there was a light in her eyes. "I remember now. I remember love. It has been a very long time since I have considered this thing." And her face contorted and she became ugly for that moment. Behind her, the Sirens shuddered at the sound of the word.

"Will you do it?" asked the princess.

"And who is it that you *love*?" She spat the word like it was poisonous.

"A Prince," responded the mermaid.

"It will do," hissed the sea-witch to her Sirens, a very satisfied expression on her face, "in fact, it is perfect."

The little mermaid had noticed that when they were still for too long, the Sirens lost their grace and appeared clumsy, as if they had not yet learned control of their massive, powerful tails. They nodded and mewed, and they appeared like a three-headed beast as they lolloped together, entwining their serpentine tails for support.

"The Prince in the castle of mountain and sea," said the witch, turning back to the mermaid.

"Yes."

"That puffed-up pretty boy. The one that cuts himself with the dagger when he thinks no one is watching," said the sea-witch to the Sirens. They nodded their heads and purred, as if they knew all along.

"And what qualifies this person, this boy," queried the sea-witch, "to be loved so much by you that you would rid yourself of your perfect form to join his wicked race?"

All of the Prince's wonders and attributes that the little mermaid had carried around within her seemed to flatten and fail. She opened her mouth to speak, but found she did not have the answer. "I don't know," she said, honestly. "Does love need a reason?"

And then, the sea-witch did a very strange thing. Her mouth stretched and extorted, and her head was thrown back as if in the process of mutation. The mermaid was alarmed – would the witch transform into a hideous creature before her very eyes? Then, a strange and haunted sound omitted from deep inside the witch.

Ha ha ha ha ha ha. Ha ha ha ha ha ha ha ha.

The Sirens joined her.

"Aren't they marvellous?" said the witch, who was now gazing at the three albino creatures fondly. "So useful, and so loyal to their mistress they would sacrifice their own limbs." And for an instant, the little mermaid saw the Sirens for what they really were: skeletal, transparent things with lifeless hair like noodles and opaque, pupil-less eyes. Like marionettes once enjoyed by children who had grown up and forgotten them, garnished with dead, sagging jellyfish threatening to slide from their faces in one greasy, comical movement. Broken dolls in their shabby bowler hats once so debonair, now pathetic. And then she saw with horror their missing pieces – ears, teeth, fingers and feet, and the great brown patches that grew from them, coated in coarse black hairs. But a second later, the vision disappeared, and the Sirens were whole again, statuesque with yellow hair entwined with poison tentacles. The little mermaid was no longer afraid of them.

"And have you told anyone – anyone at all, about this *love*?" asked the sea-witch cunningly.

"Yes," replied the mermaid, "I told my sister."

And the sea-witch nodded in great approval and smiled an oily smile. "Have you told your handsome prince?"

"No."

"No, I thought not. When was the last time you saw this person?" asked the witch thoughtfully.

"Weeks ago."

"And where did you last see him?"

The little mermaid was ashamed of the answer, although she did not know why. "He was in the water, sinking."

"He was trying to kill himself, naturally," said the witch airily.

"No!" cried the mermaid, for the thought was strange and terrible to her.

"Then what was he doing?"

"I don't know!"

"Oh, I see," replied the sea-witch, "you've told yourself that he was trying to find a way to be with you. You believe he must know you, after all, haven't you returned to his room every evening? And doesn't he play that infernal instrument for your benefit? Every action must have a reaction. You want to believe it, but you know that isn't exactly the truth, don't you?"

The little mermaid said nothing at all.

"But there is something you should know about the human race," she continued, lowering her voice as if she were conveying a deep secret, "that they are treacherous. They are betrayers and liars above all. They say they love when indeed they do not, and they run about breaking each other's hearts so often, their lives have become pathetically miniscule. Is that what you want?"

"Yes."

"So let me get this straight," said the witch conversationally. "You want to pay me an enormous fee to become close to a human, a traitorous, lying human, who does not know you love him, and in fact, loves himself so little that he recently tried to slaughter his own body. But if he does not love himself, how is he capable of loving you? For if there is one thing a human loves, it is himself."

"That's not all," cried the mermaid defensively, "I want the Immortal Soul!"

The sea-witch stopped dead and stared at her with fascination. "You are not like your sisters, are you?" she asked slowly, with intent. "In fact, you are not like any merfolk alive, are you? Haven't you always felt special – *different?*"

The little mermaid had always felt different, but never presumed herself special. So she remained silent, not wanting to taste the witch's bait. "In fact," continued the witch, "right now you are saying to yourself that out of all the people you have ever known, the person you are most like is...*me.*"

And the mermaid cried out, for it was like the very words had been snatched from her mind, and even though she did not understand, she heard the rhythmic drumming of the creature inside of her, and also the pounding of the witch's, and she knew that a parallel existed between them, but she did not want to know what.

"Bring it to me," snapped the witch, and instantly, a Siren placed in her hand a little glass bottle that contained a liquid drop, glowing golden in the dark. "This little thing," whispered the sea-witch turning the bottle over in her hand, "this is what you want? For what I have is mine, and I cannot give it to you. Even if I wanted to." And she held the bottle up to the mermaid's face, and she saw that the witch's Immortal Soul was hammering against the cork, desperate to escape. "But if I die, this would not go to heaven," continued the witch, "because there is no heaven and there is no God. And even if there were, I would go elsewhere I am sure, for all the deeds I have done."

But the little mermaid knew she was lying, for she had seen the God herself, and felt it warm her face. "I don't want your Immortal Soul," said the little mermaid defiantly, "for the Prince will give me half of his own in the ceremony of marriage."

The sea-witch smirked and shrugged. "You take a great deal of notice of what that old hag tells you. Don't be so eager to believe old wives' tales." And she uncorked the little bottle and out flew the golden drop, and the witch guided it into her mouth and swallowed it. The mermaid watched in horror as the witch began to gag, as if strangled, her face turning a shade of blue, grasping her throat with her claw. She coughed and wheezed, and out of her mouth flew a great many items: rotted flesh, old letters, a pair of feathered wings, crusty volumes of books, skulls of small animals, pieces of hair, a black onyx necklace and finally, the little golden soul. The witch pounced upon it and thrust it back in its prison, corking it with determination. "You see? It no longer wants to live in me." And she shrugged and threw the bottle into the water, where it disappeared with a flash. "I've been trying to get rid of it for years, but it follows me everywhere."

"Who are you?" asked the little mermaid, for she was sure the witch was not her kind, but could not possibly be human either.

"I am the face you will see on the day of your death," she replied customarily.

"Many other's deaths maybe," said the little mermaid, "but never mine."

She felt a surge of hatred for this woman. She hated her words and the complexity she intentionally added to an already complex situation. She did not like these new emotions, or the thudding creature inside of her, and all she wanted was to get over and done with the thing she wanted most of all.

The sea-witch, on the other hand, was astonished by the mermaid, for she had forgotten what love looked like, and she had been so anticipating smelling the stench of fear, after all these years without a single visitor. The light in the mermaid's eye scared her, for it was reminiscent of her own reflection many generations ago. But it was all a means to an end. When she laid her secret plans all those years ago, she had no guarantee of success, but her inner voice whispered assurances and it had been right: all things were coming to fruition. She had known the girl was the lock and here she was in her cavern, handing her the key. Her dark gaze flickered over the girl. She was obstinate to be sure, and wilful too. How dare she stare with such rebellion, such malevolence! What a self-righteous thing love was. It made everyone believe they were fearless. That they would live forever.

Suddenly, the witch wanted the mermaid as far from her as possible, and did not care about her outcome. It had already begun, and the mermaid's own personal quest was none of her concern. So she clapped her hands together twice. The essence of day and the powder of night, a litre of blood, two hamstrings and five toes cut from a Siren, and black ooze squeezed from the witch's breast all bubbled in a cauldron that materialised on the cavern's floor. Finally, the sea-witch descended on the little mermaid and with a sharp silver knife, pried open her jaw and sliced off her tongue in one clean sweep.

"Payment," commented the sea-witch and swallowed it whole. "I told you it would be high." And she began to laugh at her joke, and the Sirens laughed with her, for they knew no better. The mermaid's mouth filled with a raw stickiness and she tried to speak, but no noise omitted from her mouth apart from the bubbling of blood.

Ha ha ha ha ha. Ha ha ha ha ha ha ha ha ha.

"If you take this tonic," said the sea-witch, holding a bottle of a sickly grey substance, still frothing and hot to the touch, "you will never return to this world again. You will remain in human form until the Prince falls in love with you, upon which a part of his Immortal Soul will flow into your body, and you will be thoroughly human." At this, the witch suppressed another laugh. "But if the Prince does not fall in love with you, your heart will break. The moment your heart breaks, then you, like all of your beloved humans, will die. Your body will become the foam on the waves. And this is not part of the spell," she added, "it's a part of the human condition. Ironic, no?"

And the little mermaid snatched the tonic and drank it down in several, burning gulps. Her body began to heave and contort, and she could barely make out the witch's voice say, "Every step you take on land will be like daggers slicing through your feet. You will end your days standing in pools of blood." The Sirens too were chanting something, something ominous and terrible, and finally, there was no more noise, just a deep and empty silence.

When the little mermaid awoke, she opened her eyes and saw God.

Eight
ORANGES

IT TOOK TWO months to return the Prince back to the kingdom.

On that very first day of his rescue from drowning, lying on a straw-lined cot in a simple monastic cell, the Prince decided to employ a sort of amnesia, and refused to answer questions about his identity. In fact, he rather enjoyed himself, because for the first time in his life no one looked at him unfavourably when he declined opportunities of conversation. Instead the nuns, a rather stiff group of women, tittered amongst themselves and nodded their heads gravely. They would leave a bowl of gruel and a glass of water by his bed and glide out of the room, legless.

It took a great deal of time for the Prince to adjust to the meals, for it was gruel three times a day, no exceptions. However, the young novice who was on kitchen duty took pity on the boy, and would smuggle in a bit of bread, or slices of peeled orange concealed in a napkin.

The nuns had a practice of sluicing their invalids with a potent tonic consisting of menthol and vinegar that twice a day the Prince was forced to endure. He initially had panicked wildly, as the most senior group of nuns entered his chamber in a sombre fashion and rolling up the sleeves of their habits, nodded to each other and abruptly began to strip him naked. He closed his eyes in humiliation as their hands and sponges scrubbed at every inch of his body with vigour, and did not hover over or contemplate his severe latticing of scars. It was like they did not exist. It was like they were perfectly natural.

After that day, the Prince lost his fear of nakedness - no small feat, for the Prince had been bathing himself out of shame since he was fifteen. It occurred to him that a nun was an upstanding and admirable kind of woman, and he especially liked their faces beneath their wimples. He thought them all perfectly charming, even the elderly nuns that tottered in the orange grove all day long, lacking strength for their vocation. It dawned on him that in all his days at court, he had never seen so much as a wrinkle on a woman's face, or a lip that was not scarlet, or an eye not veiled with some false diffidence. The nun's faces were like canvasses to read, intricate and noble, and every crease told a tale. He enjoyed searching the younger nuns' faces and trying to guess where the lines would form.

As he lay on his straw bed, his nostrils filled with menthol and vinegar, he would listen to their voices raised in hymn, or the bells of the church steeple. At night, he would count the stars and some days it was enough to feel the sun on his body. He had hoped that perhaps some students, particularly the neat and tidy girl who had watched his resuscitation, would be sent to fetch his empty bowl. Unfortunately for the Prince, that was not the practice of this convent, where young men and young ladies should be completely segregated at all times. He could hear them sometimes, laughing in the grove, and he was sure he had never heard anything simpler in his life. Suddenly, women weren't so horrible after all.

After a short while, it occurred to the Prince that he could not spend his whole life in the convent. He could not have his body slavered with medicine every day, and neither could he live on gruel alone. The hay beneath him smelled more and more of donkey with each passing moment, and the sound of young girls' laughter was driving him wild, wilder than he thought possible in reference to females. The nuns were not his servants after all, and he felt his heart warm toward them, for they dug their own gardens to grow vegetables for the poor, and all spare alms from their weekly collection was handed to the widows.

And so the Prince recovered from his amnesia, and couriers were sent forth briskly, and news spread throughout the land. Messages were exchanged, gifts of gold arrived, and so eventually did an envoy from the Prince's own kingdom, consisting of knights and lords and the King's own brother. New clothes that now felt too heavy and too fussy were thrown over his body, his ears crammed with commiserations and inquiries. A story had been fabricated and sent to all corners of the empire, which involved kidnapping and intended assassination, given the unseemly ropes that were found near the Prince's unconscious body. A story that everyone believed except for the Uncle, who had invented it himself.

As a parting ritual, the nuns requested that the Prince and his troupe attend a single mass. They willingly obliged, and as the Prince sang the hymns and knelt and stood and exchanged the sign of peace, he found his gaze drawn to the rows of schoolgirls in the hope of glimpsing one. Several of them turned their heads during the mass to stare at him, but none of them were the ordinary girl from the beach. Disappointed, he returned to his land, and it seemed that his whole kingdom smelled of oranges.

The court of advisors launched a full-blown investigation into the abduction of the Prince, but it lost its steam and eventually fizzled out. This was primarily due to the Prince's lack of cooperation, for it seemed that these criminals had treated their monarch so violently that he did not retain any memory of the event. When it became clear to all that the happenings of that night were to remain a mystery, the advisors returned to their secret meetings and discussed earnestly whether the Prince was at all suitable for the throne, now that he was considered brain-damaged. Perhaps his memory would one day return, as do some trauma survivors, but he certainly was behaving differently.

They had seen more of him now than ever before. He no longer hid in the trees of the terrace gardens, and his Uncle was yet to prise him from the bed of his water-level chamber. In fact, he had rather astonished the governor-general just this morning, as the latter was taking his post-breakfast stroll amongst the corridors. "Good morning!" exclaimed the Prince, who had materialised out of nowhere, looking rested and amiable. The governor-general was exceedingly shocked, stammered a reply, and scurried away to tell everyone of this strange occurrence.

The Prince started to show up to half of the meetings he was required to attend, and in some instances, even appeared to be listening. Once or twice he voiced an opinion, and though it was not the most educated of opinions, neither was it nonsensical. It seemed to the court that the Prince had finally learned, or decided to remember, their names, for they found themselves addressed frequently when face-to-face. Why, he had even attended the banquet set in honour of his safe return! To think! There was the Prince himself, at the head of the table and to the right of his Uncle, standing and responding to every toast! And even though he declined to dance afterwards, for once he did not back away from the ladies when they approached him. Instead, he listened for a while, nodding his head, and sometimes attempted a wry smile, to the delight of all. Was this brain-damage? wondered the court. Some privately thought that if the Prince were indeed brain-damaged, then everyone could do with a bit more brain-damage in their lives.

The cooks of the palace were astonished when the Prince began to request oranges for his breakfast. No oranges had ever been seen in the kingdom, and only the very well travelled and the very well read understood what oranges were. Crates of the fruit were ordered from neighbouring countries, and the court became so fascinated with their juicy flesh and tangy aroma that the Prince was obliged to throw an Orange Luncheon, where the cooks made a special orange juice for the guests to sip, and mixed the oranges into the chicken salad. They diced them and arranged them on skewers, and grated the peel into cakes. The roast beef boasted an orange sauce, and garlands of orange blossom floated atop every individual dish. It was a great success, and the Prince seemed to be enjoying himself. He asked a lot of questions about the origins of the fruit, and where exactly they had been ordered from. But not one answer included the convent on the seaside.

The Uncle watched his nephew with a shrewd eye, and was greatly encouraged by the changes seen in him. He was wise enough not to ask the real version of events of that fateful night, but he was intelligent and had pieced it all together. He mourned that the Prince had been miserable enough to cast himself into the sea, but he had not seen so much as a trace of that sad character since the Prince had returned from the south of France.

Certainly, the Prince was often quiet and thoughtful, but it seemed he no longer wished to remain invisible – it seemed he had realised that he had *value*. The Prince did not smile a great deal, or converse lightly, but neither did he have that haunted, empty look in his eye. The Uncle privately rejoiced when the Prince and the little black dog finally left the sea-level chamber and resumed the King's suite on the upper floors. He did not know what to think of the latest obsession with oranges, for the Uncle had had plenty of opportunities to sample the fruit, and thought it nothing special.

In fact, the Prince was relieved to have left the sea-level. When he had returned to his bedchamber after the long absence, he sensed a forbidding morbidity inside the room. He recognised flecks of his own blood on the Persian rugs, and was afraid. He rummaged through the opulent sheets of his bed until he found the dagger and held it in his hand. He observed the instrument of pain and peace that had been his ally all of these years, and also his greatest enemy. It was small and silver, and its handle was made in the image of a great serpent. And it seemed that he watched himself now, a sunken figure slung across the bed like a rag doll, with hollows for eyes and hollows for cheeks, tracing his naked body with the dagger as his mind was pillaged by evil thoughts. When a particularly terrible idea invaded him, in plunged the knife and it sliced more at his mind than his body. Filled with disgust, the Prince hurled the knife through the open window. He stepped out of the chamber, calling the dog after him. He never returned to it again.

He took to consulting his Uncle about all manner of things, but mostly things he should have already known but did not:

"Who exactly are our allies and how many more years will the treaties last?"

"Where do the trade routes lie and is there a more efficient way of exporting our goods that distance?"

"Was the Countess really the mistress of my grandfather and should we continue to pay her annuity?"

"Why is there no clean water supply in the remote parts of the kingdom and how many wells should we build?"

All of these questions delighted the Uncle, and the Prince soon became his earnest student, and began to frequent the dinner tables of the advisors in order to listen.

Apart from that, the Prince did not socialise much and could be found all hours of the night in the library, absorbing books on a great many subjects he did not understand at first – economics, foreign trade, agriculture. When he was not in the library, he would supervise the planting of the orange grove in the far courtyard of the palace.

Still he did not openly converse with his peers, other rich boys of his age who were at court as apprentices to their lordly fathers, and neither were they terribly interested in his friendship. He made brief appearances at some balls or parties if requested to do so, but he did not dance. He listened to one or two women, and even engaged in five minutes or so of pleasurable small talk, of which he was becoming quite adept, for he found it enjoyable to discuss the weather. Indeed, the ladies of court found him irresistible – for who could not love a dark and handsome kidnapping survivor, with mysterious eyes and a thrilling voice, who was forever sucking on oranges?

The Prince was resolved to the fact that he would never know a woman, and was very happy to restrict his relations with them to a few words here and there, a smile and a nod. He was no longer afraid of them, indeed they did have some outstanding qualities, but the Prince had greater things on his mind, even if his Uncle did not. Once or twice the Prince would bump into a partially dressed maid sneaking out of his Uncle's apartments. Late at night, he would hear giggles from the chamber as he passed on his return from the library, and he swore he heard the deep groans of the Countess at five o'clock in the morning. He was beginning to realise the magnetic pull his Uncle seemed to have on women. He was always surrounded by a throng of them at parties, and would barely stand still long enough for a conversation, as he was always sweeping off one lady or another to dance. Even the maids, at mealtimes, would regard him with half-lidded eyes, as if they knew his secrets.

But the Prince was happy to permit his Uncle the lion's share, as no women at court interested him, and were unlikely to ever do so. Until one night, when the Prince had reluctantly made his way to the ballroom, for he was studying the greater arts of geometry and found it quite absorbing. His uncle had been warning him about the event all week long, more insistent that usual that he make an appearance. Grudgingly, he stood amongst the throng of people in the hall, the men in their stately finery, the women in those horrible fluffy dresses that made them appear far fatter than they really were. He stood there for a long time, not speaking to anybody, acknowledging a duke or two as they swept by. Then he saw *her*.

She was wearing a white dress, cheap and coarse and out of fashion, and she was backed up against the wall, as if the noise and the spectacle alarmed her. She was very pretty, but she wore no jewels, and could have easily passed for a maid out of uniform. The Prince experienced a spark of recognition, but it faded in a second. He did not know what on earth possessed him, but he found his feet making their way toward her. He stopped, and she looked at him, and something burst like the flash of fire, or the popping of a balloon.

"All this," said the Prince before he knew what he was saying, "it's all rather boring, don't you think?"

NINE

HOUSEKEEPING AND OTHER DOMESTIC SERVICES

HAD ANYONE WALKED by, they would have stopped and stared and maybe even laughed, for it was not common to see a young woman asleep on the palace steps, completely naked. But these steps were hardly the grand staircase, they were only the meagre little back stairs that led to the ocean, green and slippery with moss, unused and forgotten. When the mermaid awoke, the heat of the midday sun burning her skin, she instinctively threw herself back into the ocean, for it all seemed a dream. But she could no longer breathe the water, and when she brought her fingers to her neck, she found the gills had disappeared.

Elated, she struggled to kick her legs in the water to

propel her to shore, but they were not working. They were quite useless in fact, only serving to edge her along inch by inch, and she flapped her arms to hurry the process. Her head felt too heavy for her body and it kept sinking underwater, and the ocean water stung her nostrils as it spurted out. The seawater tasted foul too, and it was so damned *wet*, and she was tiring rapidly. Perhaps her sister had been right after all – what good were legs if you could not even swim a few meters?

Finally, she reached the staircase, saved by the shallowness of low tide, and with a great heave hoisted herself onto the step only to realise that she did not know where to put her legs. They slipped underneath her, and thumped against the stone and before she knew it, she had lost her balance and fell into the water again, this time ramming her hip against the rocks. Ocean water overcame her, and the mermaid spluttered, determined to try again.

This time, she curled her legs under her in a crouching position, but her feet were small and smooth and away she went, slipping on the moss. She heard a strange noise above her, like a chuckle, but nobody was there.

After a few attempts at this, the princess finally managed to crawl on her knees up a few steps to where the stone was dry. She felt sheepish moving about like this, but she convinced herself that no one would ever know. She grasped the railing and attempted to stand, but her knees buckled and she nearly fell. Steadying herself, she placed a foot on the next step and as she transferred her weight onto it, a searing pain like fire entered her. She remembered the witch's final words and knew they were no lie. She bit her upper lip with the pain and tasted her own blood, and suddenly recalled this sensation the night before and tried to feel for her tongue.

It was not there. There was something at the back of her throat, a stump perhaps, but the tongue was gone all the same. She opened her mouth to exclaim but no sound came. She tried again to form the words, but there was nothing but air. She tried to yell – nothing. The witch had swallowed her speech.

Perhaps it was all for the best. The mermaid did not know how to explain herself to the humans, or whether they would believe her. She did not know if they spoke more or less the same language, so it was a very good thing that she could not attempt speech, or she might give herself away. In fact, she was not sure where to live and what to eat, for it was certain she could not live in the water or on these steps. However, fish were plentiful on these banks and she could easily catch a few, if she could only teach herself to swim in her new form. And worst of all, she did not know how to clothe herself. All of these thoughts consumed her, which was all very well and good, because they took her mind off the pain.

As she staggered up the steps, she saw that there was a pile of something waiting on the landing. When she realised what it was, her mood instantly brightened, for surely God wanted her here to send such a gift! She sat down beside it and unfolded every item, laying them out on the dry bricks to examine them. Her very first human clothes.

There was a black dress, calf-length and plain, and a frilly white pinafore, complete with a starched apron. There was a little black cap and a pair of stockings. There was a pair of large, puffy pants, beige-coloured, with frills about the edge, and a strange contraption consisting of two cups and a wide band. There were also smart black shoes, with laces. It took a great deal of time and pain until the mermaid had assembled herself, for she did not realise at first that she was to wear all the clothing at once, and they were too many hooks and buttons. She had no idea at first that the stockings were for her legs, after unsuccessfully attempting to slide them up her arms and over her head. Her wet hair and back seeped through her new clothes. Also, the brassiere hurt her breasts and whatever it was that lay between her legs chafed against the underpants.

When she was assembled, she practiced her steps, a hand on the railing for guidance. The shoes pinched her, but she could not feel it, such was the roaring pain of her every step. She was deep in concentration when a mighty hand reached out and grasped her arm, and she let out a silent gasp as she whirled around to see an ugly, red face grimacing at her.

"Out for a wee swim on the job, are you?" thundered the face with a big wet mouth. "I'll have your job for this!"

The little mermaid spluttered and stared back at her assailant, utterly perplexed.

"Eh, what's your name then?" cried the woman. The little mermaid opened and closed her mouth rapidly, desperately seeking to convey that she could not speak. "Scared, are you?" said the woman, "Scared of losing your job? Or scared of me?" And she shook the little mermaid until she heard her teeth rattle.

"Enough!" came a voice from the hallway, and there

were loud footsteps as the woman had the sense to thrust the little mermaid away from her. She landed in a painful heap on the floor, and looked up in time to see a large, powerful man approach. With a jolt, the mermaid realised that he looked a little like her Prince, only broader and older, with the exception of what appeared to be a hairy animal growing on his face. She felt a rush of pity for him, for it must be terribly hard to exist with such a large parasite attached to the head. His brows were drawn together tightly and in his eyes was a fierce expression as he looked down upon the woman who had accosted her. Her body was bent in a strange position, head down, one foot tucked behind the other, both hands holding out the hem of her skirt. "Name and rank," demanded the gentleman softly.

The woman mumbled something, and it seemed to the little mermaid that she was quivering. "Lower Housekeeper, your Highness," stammered the ugly woman, her eyes to the floor.

"I see," said the gentleman coldly, and he turned his back on her and approached the little mermaid. A wild sort of panic began to descend on the girl as she felt the stranger's keen eyes upon her. Ignoring the pain, she staggered to her feet, wondering if she ought to bend her body the way the housekeeper continued to. But it looked difficult and was sure to hurt.

He opened his mouth to speak to her when the housekeeper wailed, "It was all her fault, Sir! Swimming in the ocean during work hours, with no business to, mind! And she's disrespectful, Sir! Too high-and-mighty to tell me her name, and me her better!"

"Silence!" commanded the man, and he looked at the

woman like one would look at a slug in the salad. "I did not realise that the palace prohibits its staff from entertaining themselves to their own amusement on their days off."

"Days…off?" stuttered the wretched woman.

"And even if it were not so, you will find that this particular staff member services the royal wing of the palace, and is therefore under the jurisdiction of the Upper Housekeeper," continued the man in a voice like ice.

"Upper…Housekeeper," stammered the poor woman.

"Be about your business then, woman! You're one to speak of laziness and procrastination. Lead by example, as my brother always used to say."

The woman regained enough wits to curtsy to the man again and scurry away. He turned to the little mermaid and smiled kindly. "First day, is it?" he inquired gently, "Better stay out of that one's way. She's a menace."

But the little mermaid could not see his smile, for it was hiding behind the animal, and she was terrified to be in such proximity to it. She wondered what she should do if it leapt off his face and attacked her.

"You had better come with me," he said with a sigh, "and I'll show you where you belong. And by the way, your apron," he continued, pointing to the white article she had tied around her shoulders, "is not a cape. It goes around your waist."

The palace was more amazing inside than she could ever had imagined. As she walked through the passages, struggling to keep up with the long strides of her rescuer, she found that the sheer magnificence of the sights helped keep her mind off the pain that ravaged every step. They passed through halls with floors that shone like silver, and stained-glass windows depicting creatures she could never have dreamed of. She gaped at the large domed ceilings of the atriums, and there were gardens in every passing courtyard, with brightly coloured land-corals blooming. The smell was heavenly.

And the people! They were every shape and size, and wore all manner of clothing. The men were astounding – so large yet graceful, with loud bellowing voices and prominent noses. She loved the way they seemed at constant invisible battle with each other, each trying to look bigger or more powerful than the other. The women were beautiful with their black-rimmed eyes and powdered skin and hair all colours, twisted into elaborate piles atop their heads. They flapped their hands, and they simpered and they laughed. The sound was enchanting. Once or twice she noticed that some girls wore the very same outfit that she did, and the thought of their uniformity as comforting.

They happened upon a great stairwell and began to ascend it. Portraits of past kings lined the walls, and the little mermaid was glad to recognise the eyes in several of the paintings. As they arose, they passed the last and final portrait and she halted. She stared up at the picture and beheld her Prince, perhaps a few years younger, bearing a sobering expression. He was dressed in riding boots and a cape, and by his feet was a little black creature. The gentleman made no comment, and stood with his hands folded patiently in front of him, until the mermaid came to her senses and hesitantly met his gaze. They fell into step again, but she threw back her head more than once to see that beloved face, with eyes that seemed to be following her.

The Upper Housekeeper was a tall, angular woman with a pinched expression and copious amounts of wiry red hair stashed under her cap. She frowned when she saw the little mermaid, but lowered herself in a deep curtsy in front of the gentleman.

"A new recruit," explained the man, and he placed his hand softly on the small of the mermaid's back to propel her forward. The mermaid blushed scarlet at the heat and unexpectancy of his touch, and lowered her eyes in embarrassment.

The Upper Housekeeper was not a stupid woman, and she registered the comely, flushing girl in front of her, and her arrival with the King's own brother (who had quite a reputation) and put two and two together. "Very well, your Highness, she responded pleasantly. "I think window duty perhaps?"

"Perhaps. Sweeping and mopping possibly, and a little dusting? Nothing heavy, mind you."

"Aye, the poor thing looks too frail for the laundry room," acknowledged the Upper Housekeeper, eyeing the mermaid sceptically.

"And when she learns the ropes, I expect to see her in service."

The Upper Housekeeper failed to conceal her shock. "In service, my Lord? Already?"

The Uncle looked amused. "Yes, my dear woman, in service to myself, the Prince, and any monarchs who deign to visit our kingdom." The creature in the mermaid's chest lurched.

"But she has no experience! Forgive me, your highness, but I have served this household for thirty years and there are certain *attributes* one must possess to be in service, attributes that take years of proven trustworthiness and diligence –"

"It is on my recommendation." The Uncle gaze pierced the Upper Housekeeper and after a moment, she nodded her head gravely.

"As you wish, my lord," replied the woman, looking over the mermaid as a prospective buyer would a racehorse.

"You will find she is utterly trustworthy," commented the gentleman, "because you see, she is completely dumb." And he turned on his heel and walked away, without as much as a second glance.

"Dumb, are you?" muttered the woman as she examined the mermaid's face. "A shame. Pretty thing, you are." And she wiped her hands on her apron like they were contaminated. "Well, you've got no baggage and you've got no clothes, I gather. Where did he find you, the street? Follow me."

And the little mermaid had no choice but to lead her poor feet on, higher and higher inside the castle, until they reached a nondescript hall lined with plain wooden doors.

"These are the servant's quarters," explained her superior, "and I know it must seem mighty strange to you to have servant's quarters so high up in the castle, and not outside of it, and so close to their Majesties and all. But this is no ordinary palace, and we find this way works best. Upper servants upstairs, lower servants downstairs. And I don't find that his Lordship minds too much either," she added spitefully, looking at the girl for a reaction. The little mermaid gave none, and stared the housekeeper blankly.

"You're not deaf too?" asked the woman. "Shake your head for no, if you hear me."

The little mermaid shook her head slowly, which satisfied the housekeeper. "Good." She withdrew an enormous ring of keys from her bodice and began to unlock the first door on her right. "This will be your room." And she flung the door open and the little mermaid stepped inside.

It was small and plain, with a narrow iron bed, a chest of drawers and a tarnished looking-glass. But there were two large windows, revealing the range of limestone mountains, and very far down below was a beautiful garden with spiny white trees containing round, orange-coloured balls. "Not exactly a sea-view," said the housekeeper, "but if you lean out the window, you can hear the ocean and the seagulls, and the like."

The little mermaid was very grateful so she turned to the woman and smiled. To her great surprise, the Upper Housekeeper blushed. "Well, I've wasted just about enough time here, I think. I'm a very busy woman and I've no time to train you now, so you'd best take the rest of the day off. I've got a daughter about your size, well, she was your size before she had six children. I'll have some of her old clothes sent up. Nothing fancy, mind," she added.

And then she was gone. The little mermaid stepped over to the window and smelled the wind, and the scent of her ancestors that rode upon it. For the first time, she thought of her father, and her sisters and of her own dear nanny, and wondered if she would ever see them again. But like the shadows of haunting worry that lie around

the circumference of our minds, there was a rancidity
the air: a cloying, acidic stench that subtly coiled in....
of her nostrils and filled her with alarm. She pushed the
unpleasantness away, for today was much too wonderful
to dwell on such things. She also felt sorry, because somewhere out there, a truant maid was surely searching for
her clothes.

And so the little mermaid began her new life upon the
understanding that one must work to survive and nothing in this world came free. No one who looked upon her
would ever imagine that she was once a princess, doted
upon and adorned, feasting all day and night upon lion-
fish eggs served in the bellies of chameleon cuttlefish.
Particularly not with her sleeves rolled up, on her hands
and knees scrubbing dirty bathroom tiles. Once completed, she threw her brush into the bucket of brown
water and stood, stretching her tired shoulders and back.
She caught a glimpse of herself in the looking-glass.

She looked like she belonged. She made a face in the
mirror, the kind of face that would have made her poor
nanny shudder. She smiled in her new security. Everybody
made faces around here. Human beings, she discovered,
could not maintain the stony, frozen expressions of the
merfolk, not for an instant. There was not a moment
where their faces remained blank. There was always a light
in their eye, and the light, like red wind, would flare into a
raging fire without notice.

She was having more trouble than she bargained for
with the language these humans spoke. Although some
words had especial meaning to her, many others were

spoken too fast and too abstractly for the mermaid to comprehend their true meaning. Some things that she ought not to, she took literally. As a result, many of her peers suspected she had some sort of brain-damage, and avoided her completely.

However, she was quickly learning to read facial expressions, and that was contributing greatly to her understanding. She enjoyed practicing in the mirror, illustrating dramatic senses such as shock, embarrassment and sadness. (In fact, this alone contributed to the general consensus of brain-damage, when a fellow maid caught her doing this upon mistakenly entering her room.) When she coupled her comprehension of expressions and her rapidly growing vocabulary, she began to partially understand the humans, which was a great comfort to her.

Indeed, a life of labour suited her well. She enjoyed the list of domestic tasks presented to her upon the arrival of a new day by the omnipresent Upper Housekeeper, and was now firmly grasping the concept of cleaning – why it must be done, and why it had to be repeated often. It was a joy to have a list of tasks to be completed in numeric order, rather than endless time of limitless leisure to face each day. There was a purpose in each day now, no matter how small or inconsequential it seemed to her peers. As a result, she excelled in her duties. There was so much to be learned, and fascination lay in every corner. There it was at the bottom of the mop bucket, where dirt and soap swirled in frothy disarray. There was fascination in the way glass shone with hidden brilliance when wiped with a damp cloth. It lay too in the cobweb-encrusted feather dusters, daddy-longlegs scurrying away, mourning the loss of their homes, eager to begin rebuilding.

The little mermaid had no pride in which to struggle through her own loss of rank. She did not have superior feelings to her fellow servants, and did not yet know how to draw comparisons. However, she sensed that there were no parallels that existed between them, and did not mind the general isolation. She noticed ungrudgingly that all occupants of the palace were there to serve their majesties. But she was the lowest of all, she realised. For it was she that had to wipe the stains from who-knows-what, and inhale the stench of God-knows-who. And it did not matter a bit.

She enjoyed being unnoticed, moving in and out of rooms with a broom or a chamber pot. She loved the time it afforded her to be alone with her thoughts, or to simply observe. There was something noble in Useful Occupation, she decided, although she did not know what. No one spoke to her a great deal, and she did not catch anyone's eye, although once or twice she found the gaze of the King's brother upon her. At these times she would smile in recognition, but he would mostly look past her and continue his conversation. Once or twice, he would raise his eyebrows or stare at her quizzically, as if he sensed she did not belong, or as if to convey that she was doing a shoddy job. The little mermaid did not relish these encounters with the gentleman. Just being in the same room with him was enough to raise an army of goose bumps on her flesh. Sometimes his stare would bring on a bout of hot flushes, and she would hide her face in shame.

She was a daytime maid, and as a result, most of the

evenings were free. The other maids were uncomfortable about her impediment, and some were jealous of the rumours concerning the Uncle. (They were a tight circle, mostly related through ties of marriage, and enjoyed robust evenings together surrounded by much laughter that echoed in the servant's quarters, from which the mermaid was largely excluded.) Sometimes she was so tired that after a meal of left-overs from the royal table, fare which caused many stomach-upsets as the mermaid was not used to cooked food, vegetables or seasoning, she would retire to her bed and sleep a good ten hours.

Roaming about the palace after hours was strictly prohibited, but the little mermaid's curiosity caused her to defy this rule, and would often skirt the empty halls, ducking from shadow to shadow, in wondrous exploration. Floor by floor, her bare feet would pad across the halls and by moonlight would discover pieces of humanity usually concealed in daylight.

Once, she observed a well-dressed couple scurrying within a darkened atrium, whispering. There was a sense of rushed anticipation in the air. They stopped outside of a door and suddenly, the woman launched herself at the man. Her arms were locked around his neck, and in a bout of pure strength, wrenched his body down to hers. His arms immediately circled her waist, and all bodily proximity was eliminated. Suddenly, the man lowered his head and placed his mouth on the woman's own. The little mermaid was filled with revulsion. Was he ingesting her? Were humans indeed the cannibalistic predators that her sisters had warned her about? But the woman did not appear eaten, indeed, she did not even seem disgusted by the man's act. In fact, she looked as if she were rather enjoying it. She made little mews of pleasure that turned the mermaid's stomach. Someone, in their tangle of human flesh, had managed to open the door and inside the room they tumbled. The little mermaid crouched in the shadows opposite their door for an hour, waiting to see more. But they did not reappear that night.

A few nights later, the self-same couple were strolling the very same corridor when the woman launched herself at the man again. The little mermaid tensed, straining to see more. But it was not the drunken, pleasure-mad lurch of before. The woman was saying something, forceful, muffled, all the while striking the man with her closed fist. On and on she went, lights glinting on her face like water. The man tried to restrain her, but he was no match for her fury. The little mermaid could see the sheen of the woman's wedding ring as her hands flayed the man. A golden blur.

On another occasion, the little mermaid was prowling when she detected the strangest smell wafting throughout the air. It was a sickening, disturbing and beautiful scent, so intoxicating that she had no choice but to follow it. She padded silently down the corridors of the upper floor until she reached the doorway of a large, squat terrace, usually used as a waiting area for the advisors before admission into the prominent conference rooms of royalty. Waiting for her eyes to adjust to the dimness, she focussed on the tiny gusts of red wind that swayed atop discreet candlesticks that were scattered upon the floor. The smell was heavily concentrated here, swirling around the room like a vengeful ghost. She began to feel light-headed.

After a moment, she collected herself and noticed with a start that the room was full of people. Instantly, she darted from the doorway and concealed herself in the shadows outside it. She berated herself for her stupidity, for now she could clearly hear the murmur of men's voices. Or so she thought. Everything was getting very muddled. She wondered if anyone had seen her but she needn't have concerned herself, for if any of the men had noticed, it would not have mattered a bit. Curiosity got the better of her, and she leaned over to peek though the doorway. A strange sight awaited.

The men were strewn upon mats all over the floor. They seemed to have lost all control over their bodies, which lolled about in an unsightly manner. Were these the proud, straight-backed men that battled each other with so much pride and dignity? the mermaid wondered. Surely not. They each nursed a long wooden pipe, sucking from it from time to time. From their mouths exhumed smoke dragons with long, thorny tails, which lolloped about the room chasing each other. After a time, the dragons grew tired of this game, and dissolved into thin air, letting the younger dragons run ragged in the room. The little mermaid watched all of this blankly, for she was beginning to feel sleepy, and though she had tried to rouse herself from the spot, her body felt it were made of bricks.

She did not know how she managed to drag herself to bed, but when she woke she was in her chamber, fully dressed with her shoes still on. She could have sworn that the gentleman had been present on the terrace, a man with a live parasite feeding off his face.

After this uncanny experience, the little mermaid

refrained from exploring the palace at night. She had a vague sense that she had witnessed something she ought not to, and a little darkness had crept into her that she did not know how to expel. The Lower Housekeeper had been seen frequently monitoring the halls, and the mermaid did not wish another encounter with her.

From then on, her evenings were blissfully spent down at sea-level. As the God disappeared into the ocean, bathing everything in a glorious hue, she would slowly descend the old stone steps that led to the sea, barefoot. Little rivulets of blood seeped from her soles and between each toe, and she would ease herself into a sitting position, lift her skirts, and place each foot gingerly into the warm seawater. She would lean back and remember her family and sometimes, she would hear the crooning of the melancholy music overhead.

During this time, the little mermaid lived off the hope and love that was by now so infused with her being. She had not seen the elusive Prince, although once she thought she heard his voice as a group of men passed by, all in long black robes and in such a rush that the mermaid could not tell one from the other. She knew which suite belonged to him, the magnificent rooms in the highest steeples of the palace, yet found she had not the time to frequent the entrance in hope of a chance encounter. She had not yet been allocated the privilege of serving food or beverages, so her fraternisation with human beings apart from other servants was limited.

She was a patient girl, and would have perhaps lost hope if it weren't for the bunch of land-corals, *flowers* as the humans called them, that appeared in her mouth-wash glass every Tuesday. Each week they were different, mismatched and ill-arrayed, plucked with the undistinguishing eye of a person who knew little about floral arrangements. But the mermaid had never received a gift in her life, and she kept them long after they lost their colour and began to smell like sink-mould.

The other evidence that the little mermaid was neither alone nor friendless was the movement she often detected outside of her doorway. The servant's hall remained dimly lit all night long, and through the sliver between the door and the floor, she would see a shadow moving, disturbing the light. Once, she fancied she heard breathing. Another time, the pacing of a nervous person, contemplating knocking. It was either the Prince, the mermaid decided, or one of the witch's Sirens, spying with milky eyes, its remaining limbs dangling sickeningly as it attempted to crouch outside her door. Either way, she was not afraid.

Therefore, time that could have been spent moping or devising strategies to stumble across her beloved's path was spent in the pure relish of humanity. Despite the gnawing pain in her feet, which she was rapidly growing accustomed to and would occasionally forget, her body was something that she enjoyed exploring and testing. Her legs could move faster than a mere walking pace, she discovered, and along the barren halls at midday, she would test this practice. As she ran, the pain was excruciating yet it was exhilarating to create her own wind. It was difficult at first to master the simple art of sitting, as she was prone to becoming unbalanced, and feared she would simply topple over. She would sit on the edge of her bed in the early morning for an hour, practicing. She enjoyed breathing, as deeply as she could. She loved stretching herself horizontally on her bed and not feel gravity lift her up.

There was something strange about her body now that she were human. It was not the legs, it was what lay between them. It reminded her, at first sight, of the parasite growing on the King's brother's face, although not as large or dense. She wondered if it were alive because when she poked at it timidly with her finger, it lurched. She was careful not to touch it again.

One morning, she woke with dull pains laced along the lower curve of her belly. Upon closer examination, she found that her underwear was spotted with blood. Alarmed, she searched her body for a wound but found nothing. And so she slipped off the underwear and ran to find the Upper Housekeeper.

Upon presentation of the soiled underpants, the Upper Keeper looked at the mermaid sharply and exhaled a long, aggravated sigh. She said a great many words on the subject, much of which was unintelligible, wagging her finger at the girl as if it were all her fault. The Upper Housekeeper disappeared into her own room and brought out a pile of thick cotton napkins and made a great show of demonstrating what they were for and where they were meant to go. Many of the staff were awake by now and exiting the corridor, and they stared and clutched each other and laughed. The little mermaid returned sheepishly to her room, her eyes on the ground, clutching the napkins to her chest as if they were a shameful secret.

It took days until she recognised that the bleeding had something to do with the animal that lay between her legs, and acting accordingly.

TEN
SOMETHING METALLIC, LIKE BARNACLES

IT TOOK SOME time before the six remaining princesses realised their youngest sister had disappeared permanently. Most were unconcerned, even when it was suggested that she had likely been killed for her beauty, as food became harder to catch and therefore more expensive. It was known that the youngest was a wanderer, and not like the rest of them, and if she were stupid enough to enter gypsy territory without protection, there was nothing anyone could do. But royal body parts arouse suspicions, as the eldest pointed out, and if this had been the case, reports would have been circulating all over the kingdom by now. The mermaids nodded their heads in agreement and decided that like their mother before them, their sister had simply disappeared before her time. This explanation sat well with them, and they resumed sucking their oysters and admiring their reflections in the looking-glass.

The nanny was not convinced. She continually reminded the princesses of the youngest's obsession with the human world and the Prince that lived there. But the sisters could not connect this fact with her disappearance, and merely shrugged. They had already forgotten her. All excepting the sixth sister, who shivered at the mention of the Prince. She recalled the light that flared in the youngest's eye like a beacon and shuddered. The word that she had uttered, that one fateful word, began to echo in her head tunelessly. Nausea overcame her. She looked down at her oyster in disgust and discarded it.

From that day forth, her appetite eluded her. She tried to busy herself with her appearance, but found that it all seemed empty. Watching her sisters' stony faces as they pulled and prodded at each other with beautifying instruments of torture, she saw vanity. Watching them feast on the cold, fat bellies of porpoises, she saw waste. She did not know what these ideas meant, but her reality continued to shift throughout the final days of her life, as the poisoned thickened and virus multiplied in her bloodstream.

The sixth princess took to surveying the kingdom, and therefore began to question it. She felt stabs of compassion and horror when she saw merfolk with missing limbs, sawn off in exchange for food. She felt sorry for the hideous sea-gypsies as they were shunned by the commoners, who refused to exchange their fish even for handfuls of silvery scales. When she witnessed the slow, mundane rhythm of the simple, predictable events in a mermaid's lifetime, she asked if there was a greater purpose. The black, empty space inside of her whispered that there was. There she would stop, because the fact that she was feeling anything at all, let alone hearing voices, alarmed her.

But most of all, she wondered about love. It took hours to fall asleep at night, because the subject kept her mind racing. Finally, she stopped sleeping altogether and let the word resonate within her, her thoughts treading any path they wished to go. The small streak of humanity that was unable to be bred out of the merfolk had grasped onto the idea of love and hungered to gnaw it to the bone. There was a link somewhere, she knew, as her dead heart yearned for answers to the questions: what is love? Where is love? Where can I find it? Is all emptiness without it? And after many nights, a cold, cursed fist grasped at her heart and squeezed until suddenly, it began to beat.

Every drum of the creature inside her caused the princess to become wracked with fear. Every beat stirred the infection in her blood. She ceased all activity and took to counting the beats of her heart until she knew precisely how many there were in a day. A variation of this figure would cause her to enter a blind panic, where her body would jolt inexplicably and she would think of nothing but death. That is, nothing but love and death. And what came after death. If she found love, her heart would whisper to her in the still of night, perhaps she could gain an Immortal Soul.

She grew so sick, so grey of skin that her now-scarlet veins began to protrude through it, like sinewy rivers of poison, that the nanny and the fifth princess were sent to aid her. "Love is killing me," she hissed. "Help me find relief."

As soon as the word left her lips, it hung suspended in the air. Her closest sister tried to shy away, but it was too late. She breathed it in and it entered her bloodstream. The nanny was too old to realise that a transmission had taken place. All she knew was that there was a strange smell in the chamber, the smell of human land-corals.

All day long and well into the night, the princess writhed and moaned in her chamber, and the words she whispered were either the numbered beats of her heart, or that dreaded word that had contaminated her so. She was enclosed in fear and wonder, and finally she gave up the tale of the youngest sister, and her intention of visiting the sea-witch.

A vile, terrible beating sound filled her chamber and no one was permitted to enter except for the nanny, who had a certain tolerance for the sound. The terror of her presence cast a gloomy shadow over the palace and its inhabitants. After a fortnight of such occurrences, the mermaid's heart, so swollen with new ideas and revelations, exploded and she died.

Now the fifth sister was unmarried, unlike the eldest sisters, although she had been betrothed to a particular merman since she was an egg. Her sisters' husbands did not spend a great deal of time with their wives, as they had certain obligations to the Sea King, which included the counting of wealth and the acquiring of treasures. However, it was customary that in the year prior to marriage, the betrothed couple were to spend time together, simply conversing. It was an old custom, dating back to when merfolk were more human than animal, but as time went by it became a test of fortitude. For conversing was no easy matter between mermaid and merman, and folk did not generally talk without a topic of great urgency, importance or necessity. They did not converse for conversation's sake. It was not possible.

As a result, couples merely spend copious amounts of time gazing at each other blankly. It was a pointless, tedious exercise, and usually the couple were sick of the sight of each another by one year's end. Thus was its purpose, for it was an old proverb in the kingdom that:

> "Those who small-talk for a year
> won't then leave those who they hold dear".

One day, after her sister's death, the fifth princess's betrothed came to call. As usual, they retired to an isolated chamber, one with a breathtaking view of the kingdom, which usually helped inspire topics of conversation. But today was a particularly dry day, as the merman had run out of previously-planned comments within the first hour. As the pair gazed at each other, the fifth princess found that her gaze was not so blank, after all. She began to study her betrothed in great detail. She noted his noble forehead and clear eyes. He had a strong jaw and a head full of gloriously long hair. His tail was strong and muscular, and gleamed green. His torso was well-defined and he had large pectorals with very smooth, very pink nipples. He was a handsome specimen as was expected, for he was very rich. If she had always known that he was beautiful, then why had she never *noticed*? Why he was suddenly so attractive to her?

The fifth princess was filled with an unfamiliar feeling of curiosity. She wondered what would happen if she touched his skin. The thought of it brought tingles to her spine and gingerly, she edged closer to her betrothed. The merman sensed her advance and began to grow alarmed. This was certainly odd behaviour. What on earth was she doing? Instinctively, he began to back away, trying to maintain the same proximity between their bodies. But the fifth princess was surprised at the pleasure she felt in pursuit of him, so she accelerated her pace and soon she had cornered him.

His eyes swung wildly in their sockets as he sought escape. But the princess was strong and slowly, she drew out her hands and placed them softly on the merman's chest. The merman calmed a little, and watched in wonder as the mermaid began to stroke his body slowly and deliberately. A slaving of goose-pimples erupted all over his flesh. He was mesmerised. She, on the other hand, was astonished that his skin felt just like her own. She wondered why she had not thought to do this earlier. It was so much more interesting than small-talk.

The streak of humanity that had been ignited in the princess burned quickly as she found her face drawn toward his own. He had an engaging mouth, she realised, and was insatiably curious to taste it. Without further hesitation, she gripped his forearms and placed her mouth gently over his own. Not knowing how to proceed, she held it there.

The merman, who had seen his fair share of predators

and was an avid hunter, was absolutely frozen with perplexity. In the mere seconds it took for his betrothed to advance, his mind had formed an intricate escape plan, which he was now strangely reluctant to act upon. There he remained, attached to the mermaid at the mouth, and suddenly his stomach twisted inside him and he felt rather curious. She was not going to eat him, he decided, and she was not going to attack further. Odd as it was, there was something pleasant in this act, this simple brushing of the lips, and before the merman realised what he was doing, old human instinct erupted.

He moved his lips beneath hers and opened his mouth. She tasted the smooth saline of octopus ink, and a hint of something metallic, like barnacles scraped from the hull of a sunken ship. Heat filled her body as she understood there was more of his mouth to taste, to explore, and time stood still. Her dead heart began to burn inside of her, and suddenly, it lurched and began to beat.

The next day, the merman arrived at the palace earlier than usual, and he and the fifth princess retired to their chamber where they immediately resumed their bodily exploration of the other. There was more to discover this time, and soon it became habitual. The merman would stay long into the night, and sometimes would not bother to leave the palace at all. He would sleep with his tail entwined around his betrothed, and wake to resume their feverish rubbing. A deadly, throbbing sound filled the chamber and no one would dare enter. It terrified all inhabitants of the palace.

One day, the fifth princess turned toward her betrothed and asked, "Do you love me?"

As soon as the word left her lips, the merman greedily breathed it into his nostrils, and it smelled like perfume. There the word lodged itself into the wide, gaping pores of the virus, lying dormant and peaceful in his bloodstream, and he became feverish with infection. "Of course I do," the merman replied, and he meant it.

Their remaining days were spent in that chamber, which became a blessed sanctuary to them. They refrained from eating and sleeping, utterly consumed with love for the other, understanding that every moment not spent in exploration of the other was a moment wasted. The remaining four princesses became aware of their deaths only when the fateful beating in the chamber ceased. When they carefully entered the room to survey the damage, they held their noses, for the sickening smell of flowers pervaded everything. The room was empty. There was an imprint on the floor, of two bodies entwined like they were one flesh.

When the Sea King realised that his daughters were dying, a paralysing fear captured him. He avoided contact with them in the hopes of preserving his life, and did not wish to know further information about the virus that was sweeping the kingdom. He was resentful of the rumours that the disease originated within his very walls, and did not believe it, as everyone knew that disease and all manner of foul things came from close fraternization with sea-gypsies. Strange sensations seemed to follow him, the taste of an expensive potion, the silk of black hair against his cheek, the icy, beautiful reflection in the looking-glass. Sometimes, it seemed as if an animal had taken residence inside his ribcage, a small, feathered creature that would stretch its wings and flutter within him. It was a horrify-ing sensation.

Occasionally, these occurrences would remind him of the youngest princess. He vaguely recalled that she had disappeared sometime previously, but tried not to dwell on it. Thoughts about the youngest were always rimmed with black ooze, and the Sea King was loathe to recall her origins. However, there was a link that forged his youngest daughter indistinctly to the disease, but he did not know what.

The nanny in vain sought audience with the Sea King, who refused her admittance. She was old and wise, and committed herself to isolating the disease and discovering its cure, in her own small way. But the princesses would not hear talk of it and shunned her, suspecting her to be a carrier. The fourth sister had recently taken ill, and took to muttering numbers and lying in her back with her fingers prodding the thing hammering within. The nanny knew her time had come when the layers of ice that had stilled her own heart suddenly cracked and it began to beat.

As the forth princess and the nanny lay together dying, the remaining sisters called a meeting. Clearly there was a contagious disease present in the palace, but unlike scale-rot and leprosy of the gills, there seemed no immedi-ate cure nor apparent prevention. Rumours had reached the palace that the disease had puckered within the noble community and had even reached the sanctuary of the commoners. Several people had confined themselves to their homes and it seemed that everyone was debating the forbidden word, this new idea, with a passion they never knew they had.

And so the remaining three princesses, each with the virus curled passively inside them, talked and talked, pooling their memories, until at last they realised that their very youngest sister, the strange one who had forsaken their species, was their only hope. She had defied the boundaries of their existence. She had been brave enough to consult the sea-witch, and who knows what powers had been granted to her there? There had always been a strange essence stirring within her. Perhaps there was a cure in the human world that she could bring to them.

The little mermaid was ritually bathing her feet, watching with fascination the blood clouding the water, when on the horizon three familiar faces appeared. She squinted and shielded her eyes from the light, as three heads bobbed up and down in the waves, their eyes searching vigilantly for predators. They waited until the sun had entirely set before timidly approaching, and the mermaid restrained herself from jumping into the water and wrapping her arms around them. She grinned at them, and motioned for them to come closer. The sisters looked at each other in confusion at their sister's unrestrained facial expressions. Something about it hurt them.

"Oh sister," said the eldest, "why have you come to this terrible place? We know of your bargain with the sea-witch and that you can never return. Tell us that you regret your decision and we will make a great payment to bring you back."

But the little mermaid shook her head sadly.

"Oh sister," said the second-eldest, "why won't you

speak? Will you not converse with your own flesh and blood? We have travelled a long way to hear your voice."

But the little mermaid shook her head furiously, and patted her throat firmly, decisively. She pointed to the waves. Although the princesses were not used to sign language of any sort and were not inventive by nature, after much consultation with each other, they finally understood.

"Oh sister," they said, "why have you traded your beautiful voice for this lonely life? You will die here, dried out by the sun. This world reeks of dead things. Everything is so ugly."

"Don't you remember how wonderful our kingdom is?" moaned the eldest. "The lights, the pearls, and all the good things to eat. Don't you remember your own fish's tail? And now you have two stumps, mutilated like a sea-gypsy."

But the little mermaid could only smile at their admonitions, so ludicrous they seemed. When the sisters found they were getting nowhere, they changed tactics.

"The sea-witch has a spell that can bring you back."

A bolt of loathing surged through the little mermaid. She leapt to her feet and mouthed the words "She is a liar!" in her native tongue.

"Oh sister," said the third princess, who was beginning to feel dizzy from the array of emotions displayed, "haven't you heard the news? For we are all that is left of the Sea King's beautiful daughters. Our other sisters are dead. And so is our dear nanny."

The thing that lived inside the little mermaid began to thunder, rapidly.

"It started with the smaller one, the closest to you in age. It has been said that something caused her heart to beat. Everyone knows a mermaid's heart is not supposed to beat. Every night, her chamber would be filled with a horrible, drumming sound. But no one knows what caused it."

The creature inside the little mermaid's chest contracted and began to moan a still, sad song.

"After she died, the fifth sister followed," the eldest continued. "She and her betrothed would lie in their chamber all day and all night, *touching* each other. It was very odd. In a matter of days, the fourth became infected too. Everyone is dying, sister. Although the nanny matters little, as she was meant to die soon in any case."

"Will you come back with us? Will you help us?" they cried in unison, their blank eyes blinking rapidly, their white skin turning grey in the cold moonlight.

But the little mermaid knew that she could not. She did not know why her family was dying, and there was an unpleasant sensation at the back of her mind that pointed its knobbly, accusing finger at her. She shied away from it, and pushed it down into the deep recesses of her being. Having to return to the neon kingdom filled her with horror, and to enter into another deal with the sea-witch was a nightmarish thought. The witch would demand payment, and take whatever she had left. Besides, didn't she say that the spell was irreversible? The little mermaid did not want to go back. To say goodbye to the Prince forever, when she had yet to say hello.

So she looked at the empty faces of her sisters and steeled her will. The heavy gravy of guilt filled her and the mermaid made up her mind all over again. Her eyes stung mysteriously as she shook her head a final time. Their mission failed, the mermaids abandoned their youngest sister, without saying goodbye or expressing regret, for this was not their way. However, when the others had already ducked their heads underwater, the eldest turned to the little mermaid and said, "The very air of this world is filled with the beating of a thousand hearts. It is enough to make anyone sick."

Every night since, the little mermaid would gaze out to sea until all turned to darkness and hope that once more her sisters would appear and bring her news. But they did not come back.

Often she fell asleep in the frozen peace of those evenings. Sometimes she would wake with the white moon staring down at her, like the engorged, pupil-less eye of a Siren. She would drag her numb feet wearily up twenty or so floors to her room. Other times still, she would wake up in her own bed and wonder if she dreamed the whole thing.

The sea-witch regretted that she had ever heard the rumour. Sometimes she mused that the beings and all they promised were a trap, preying on foolish, withered souls and damning them to a different kind of hell. Or perhaps she ought to have listened when they told her not to trust her broken heart. For it had deceived her in the end, and here she was in limbo. Perhaps she should have, in her youth, listened to her father when he begged her to practice rationality. Perhaps she should have thought through her request. Perhaps she ought to have taken it back. But most of all, she wished that she had never found the beings in the first place, and that they had simply let her drown.

It had been wonderful, those very first decades. The solitude, the darkness. The gradual accumulation of her powers. She had crossed the ocean many times over, conversing with whichever sea creature would dare to speak with her, as most considered her an abomination and were afraid. After these limited occasions, the sea-witch began to yearn for companionship.

It was a delightful day for the sea-witch when she discovered the freshly dead bodies of three beautiful sisters lying on the ocean floor, close to the gorge. They were pale as ice, as their lungs had burst not twelve hours before. Already, the fish had eaten the eyes out of their sockets. The sea-witch bared her teeth and brought the bodies to her cavern, where she began to experiment. Her own dark blood was extracted and poured into the mouths of the victims. She sliced the shining black scales from her own fins and stuffed them into their empty eye sockets. And as the girls began to writhe on the ocean floor, their bodies transforming in a hideous dance and the breath of artificial life freezing the ventricles of their beatless hearts, the sea-witch vowed that she would never again donate her own precious body parts to a spell. And so the Sirens were birthed.

The Sirens were clever, for in their previous life they had been daughters of an illustrious poet, and hence, spoke only in rhyme. They were deeply attached to the sea-witch, always aiming to prove their worth and their loyalty. When the witch mentioned the great warrior jellyfish that would ride in schools thick as walls, asinine in appearance yet so deadly with their ribbons of death, the Sirens endured great pain to capture the kings of these tribes, attaching them to their heads. And there they would sit, stripped of their menace, unfed and in great pain, until all their poison leaked away, their electricity nothing but short-circuits. Still, the Sirens sacrificed their own limbs willingly for their mistress's brews, for the sea-witch was kind to them, and always made potions to grow the appendages back. But lately the witch had become complacent, deciding that the growing back of limbs was not worth the effort, as her spells became more and more infrequent.

It was some time before the idea of creating a species out of herself occurred to the sea-witch. Yet occur it did, and she was initially delighted by the companionship of what she referred to as the "perfect living specimens". The merfolk were a beautiful and highly intelligent species, incapable of deception or guile, all of the traits the sea-witch found indispensable. All day long and well into the night, the witch and her creations would discuss all manner of high and lofty subjects, and she was, at last, satisfied. She forgot her betrayal, and that there was ever such a thing as love.

The sea-witch became very active in her forged community. It was she that used her human knowledge to create the merfolk's economy and social system. It seemed only right that beauty was the key to the industry, and the sacrificing of beauty to buy possessions seemed only fair to her evolving mind. Lack of beauty equalled loss of status, for the sea-witch, lost in the hard brilliance of the ocean world and in her own arrogance, grew to detest ugliness and commonality.

When the merfolk began to grow in numbers, Mother Nature interceded. She had always been stronger than the sea-witch, and the merfolk population began to expand by natural means, without the witch's influence. Nature caused attraction to be born, and with it, all the human characteristics of devotion, faithfulness and ultimately, love. The sea-witch was thrown into a frenzy of jealousy and loathing. She detested affection. She hated the soft light in her creation's eyes. She was revolted by the blissful couplings that surrounded her, especially the males who were forged to their mates for life, never to wander, never to stray.

Thus, the sea-witch outlawed love. Initially, the merfolk were resistant. But as a pliant people, easily mastered by the whims of their maker and unable to deceive, they abandoned love, as did the generations that followed them, until it became nothing but a memory to the very oldest citizens.

When love became forbidden in the merfolk race, all of the things that sprung from it, such as expression, opinion, thoughtfulness and ownership, died with it. And all of the things that accompanied its nemesis hatred, such as envy, maliciousness and murder, died too. And thus, the great plane of humanity that made up half of the merfolk's essence was wiped away, and the species eventually evolved to become mostly animalistic. After a thousand years had passed, the word "love" was forgotten, and the sea-witch was once again at peace.

However, the sea-witch was not a rational woman,

and began to grow restless. She was tiring of the merfolk, who had lost all of their miraculousness and wonder. With the eradication of their human traits, the merfolk had become predictable, dry and boring. They no longer had the intellect nor inclination to discuss anything. All they wanted to do was eat, sleep and admire themselves. There were no clashes of will, no disagreements, and nobody questioned anything anymore. The merfolk considered themselves what the sea-witch had initially declared, the perfect race, and saw no need to improve upon perfection. And so the sea-witch withdrew from her creation, anointing a royal family to rule over an already-orderly people, and retreated with her beloved Sirens into her cave.

Every day she longed for an end to her monotonous existence. Every day she handed the Sirens her knife, commanding them to plunge it into her broken heart. But the Immortal Soul clung to her and refused to depart. And so the sea-witch tucked her pride away and returned to the gorge, where she was admitted by the beings.

They regarded her with their sceptical eye as she stood before them, in that place in the core of the earth, where time does not exist.

"I retract my wish," she said. "Please erase me, and all that has happened, from the world."

But the beings opened their single mouth, and the sea-witch saw a mountain of a million teeth, sharp and gleaming. "It is too late," they said. "It has gone too far. To erase what has occurred beneath these waters these past thousand years would be to erase the past, the future, and snap all the infinite threads that sew the universe together."

"I don't care about the universe," hissed the witch, "just let me die."

"The creator cannot die whilst the creation remains living," professed the beings in their unanimous voice.

The sea-witch smiled and ran a tongue over her lips. "And if I were to kill them, every last one of them, would I then die?"

There was a silence in the darkness. Finally, they replied, "We are not God, and hence we do not know the future," and turned their back.

"Wait!" cried the sea-witch, as the beings began to disappear, "How is it possible to kill an entire race of creatures? Am I to murder every one of them in their sleep? It would take hundreds of years!"

"All good things come to those who wait," whispered the beings.

"Stop!" called the witch desperately.

But the beings had all but vanished, except for the smallest of them all, who extracted itself from its companions and with the voice of a little girl, hissed, "Use the child. Bring humanity back."

It was then that the sea-witch remembered her daughter, the half-formed mass of fluid and sodden flesh that she had extracted from her womb in the earliest days of transformation. Then, she had stowed it away in a sealed flask that sat on an invisible shelf, next to the bottle containing her Immortal Soul. There the foetus had remained, forgotten, all of these years.

Thus, an intricate plan brewed in the witch's mind, a plan that yielded hundreds of years of painstaking patience, and the selection of the perfect monarch, cuckolded into becoming the oblivious paternal figure for her human child.

And as the three daughters of the Sea King returned to their dying kingdom that day, the sea-witch sniggered at their failed attempt of bringing the youngest back. The damage had been done, and the witch had no further use for her. So she sat by her cauldron and dreamed of pleasant things: darkness and emptiness and peace. Solitude and expiry. The Sirens flocked around her and rubbed her old, aching flesh with their mutilated nubs of limbs. The sea-witch, in turn, murmured endearments to her faithful servants. How remarkable they were.

Eleven

AT LAST

APPARENTLY THE MUSIC was deceiving. On the occasion that the little mermaid was in close enough vicinity to hear it, it often eluded her as she followed the maze of the palace to find the Prince. Sometimes it trickled down to her from above, and she would search the upstairs passages only to become lost and disoriented. Sometimes it seemed to be just outside her window, in which case she would lean out as far as she dared, but see nothing.

The music tended to evoke more than admiration for the Prince and his talents. It often reminded her of her father and the vacant, hollow expression in his eyes. She remembered the tale of how his wife disappeared many years before, and wondered about her. She thought of her dear dead sisters, especially the second-youngest and the very last words she had spoken to her – words of warning.

Something inside of her would stir and she felt a cloying, lonely sadness.

The Prince's music grew more and more rare as the days went by. In her ignorance, she had thought that music was exclusive to the Prince, as if it were a rare personality trait, a birthright. However, the little mermaid soon discovered that there was more to music than what she initially understood. That it could be produced from any possible source. She began to hear snippets of it everywhere, the humming of a tune under someone's breath, or the breeze of a symphony inside a populated hall.

Music, it seemed, could appear in many voices, and had all of the emotions and array of vocabulary as a human. It could cultivate a gradual sadness which she would plunge into, a mournful vortex. Or it could evoke giddiness, joy and a sense of gratefulness for life and its blessings. Sometimes, overhearing a particular orchestral symphony, she saw the wall that separates this world from the next lift its heavy curtain, and for one prolonged second, she understood the mysteries of life and existence.

There were a great many festivities in the palace these days, and although the little mermaid was not fortunate enough to serve inside one, she imagined what it must be like to be drowning in music.

One afternoon, returning to her room early due to an upset stomach (another tale to be sure, as our heroine had taken a great liking to the inhabitants of a rather exotic aquarium that was installed in a smaller atrium. She recognised the array of sea-creatures as the delicacies she and her sisters had so enjoyed, and did not hesitate to snack on one or two whenever she ventured by) the little mermaid found an extraordinary thing sitting on her bed.

It was a card, gilt-edged and its obtuse manner of elegant writing confused the little mermaid, who could not fathom its meaning. Hastily, she brought it to the Upper Housekeeper, who eyed it with irritably.

"Oh yes," said she, furrowing her eyebrows, "one of the ladies must have dropped this in the hall. Why are you shaking your head like that, girl? Of course she must have! Oh, don't look at me like that. I suppose your parents never taught you to read. Neither had the time or the money, I'd wager. No matter. It's not likely you'll be reading bedtime stories to anyone."

She put on her spectacles and held the card an arm's distance from her and read aloud, "The Prince and Prince Regent cordially invite – oh, it's addressed to the Countess, you know, the fat one - to the Governor's Ball, Grand Ballroom, Sea-level at eight o'clock on the eve of the twenty-third." The Upper Housekeeper cleared her throat and the card disappeared inside her bodice. "That's tonight."

The little mermaid reached out her hand to reclaim the card but the Upper Housekeeper slapped it away. "Enough of that. You'll get your turn. A few more weeks and I'll put you up for service." She gazed at the mermaid quizzically. "Eh, you're a strange lass. You certainly make us all...nervous." And she bustled off.

The little mermaid was not sure whether she liked the Upper Housekeeper. She was preferable to the Lower Housekeeper to be certain, and it was kind of her to donate two baskets of her daughter's clothing. She was not one to hover over her workers on the job, and neither was she one to nag. But she had made no attempt to fraternise with the little mermaid since that very first day, and did not relish their short moments of conversation. All matters considered, the little mermaid certainly did not hold her in high enough esteem to be kept away that night.

Returning to her room, she rummaged through the closet for her favourite dress. It was white, and she liked it because it reminded her least of the uniform she was required to wear daily. She slipped into it and stood in front of the looking-glass. The mermaid had not been around human females long enough to know that a generous period of time was customary for a woman to beautify herself. Instead, she dipped her hands into the wash basin on the dresser and smoothed them over her face. Her hair woefully lay in tangles over her shoulders. She wished she had one of those things that resembled a sea-urchin with which to brush it. Instead, she raked her fingers through it hastily. Something inside of her chest began to pound heavily.

Her mind began to ask her an array of questions she had few answers to. What would she do if she met the Prince? How could she tell him everything she had sacrificed in order to be with him? What if one of the servants recognised her? What was he really doing in the boat that night? There was another fear, a deeper fear that purred like a sleeping dragon beneath the fractured pattern of thoughts, but she let it lie. She kept her eye on the mouthwash glass.

The Grand Ballroom was located at sea-level and was a magnificent room, surrounded by glass walls that gave a panoramic view of the ocean. The guests watched the horizon as the moon climbed higher in the cloudless sky, and drank champagne. The orchestra tuned their instruments and began to play. Laughter grew louder and the guests began to dance with abandon. The staff busily tried to remain unseen as ladies wove between them, their painted eyes on some gentleman or another, as if such things as servants did not exist. All around the little mermaid, wet, sticky mouths opened and closed rapidly, like schools of baffled fish.

Then she saw him.

He was taller than most, and though he did not dance, he moved through the crowds with a certain grace. His eyes scanned the room, seeing nothing. His gaze was hooded and guarded. He was more beautiful than any creature she had ever seen. She had forgotten hair could fall like that. The creature in her chest stopped beating. The room froze and the music ceased.

He had seen her. He was coming closer, and there was a light in his eye, a light that had not been there before. The cloak of darkness, of infinite sorrow that had reluctantly trailed after him in the past, was gone. She tried not to stare, to divert her gaze – look at that woman's hat, who is that gentleman with the big hooked nose? – until he was standing in front of her. She raised her eyes to meet his and something snapped in the atmosphere. Her organs, her pores, every follicle from which sprouted hair, each muscle, each individual blood cell, even the rind in her ceaselessly growing toenails sighed deeply and breathed: *at last*.

The Prince seemed to forget what it was he wanted

to say and looked baffled for a moment. He recovered quickly and quipped, "All this, it's all rather boring, don't you think?"

The little mermaid was dumbfounded and stared at him, trying to gauge his meaning. What was this word, *boring*? Was it a positive or negative thing? Did he think that she was boring? And his eyes were black, black like the night, so dark she could not see the pupil.

"Forgive me," said the Prince. "Perhaps you find this all very diverting. I'm sorry to insult, but what's the use of being a Prince if you cannot find fault in your own party?"

The sound of his voice was so unlike the music he played. His arms looked unnatural, stiff at his sides. She could not fathom his meaning. He spoke too quickly, and his expressions changed so rapidly she could not tell which one was real.

"What's your name?" he asked.

She looked into his eyes and shook her head slowly, reaching up a shaking hand to pat her throat gently.

"You can't speak? Were you born that way?"

She shook her head again.

"Well," he said, looking at ground, "I am sorry for you."

She gave him a wary smile, for she was unsure why he should be sorry.

"Where is your family? I would like to meet them."

But the little mermaid's face fell, and she shook her head. There was something strangely familiar about this girl, and she seemed so foreign and out of place in this glittering, raucous world that he was reminded of the oldest nuns in the orange grove, the useless ones whose vocations had outgrown them. He recalled those esteemed women, and the delight on their faces as his men presented them with bags of gold, gold to hire workers to spare their brittle backs the planting and digging. Gold to share with toothless orphans and slack-breasted widows. Gold to give a second chance to a lonely child, perhaps a child just like the neat and ordinary girl that had watched him so quietly from the shore. Something inside of the Prince, something beyond pity, awoke.

And so he began to talk like he had hardly talked before, all about his kingdom, his subjects, and the fruit he was so recently besotted with. The little mermaid understood only a fraction of what he said, but she smiled when he smiled, and raised her eyebrows in astonishment when he leaned toward her to mention something especially curious, and once, when he was particularly excited, his hands flapping round and round, a lock of hair falling into his eyes, she laughed.

Ha ha ha ha ha ha ha ha. Ha ha ha ha ha ha ha ha.

Instantly, she clapped her hands over her mouth, mortified. What was the sound that had just escaped her? It was ugly, hideous, and she remembered the last time she heard it and shuddered. And the way it had rippled out of her throat, unbid and unwelcome, like surprise vomit. Why was the Prince looking at her like that? Why were people turning around to stare?

The Prince looked at her sternly. Aware that his guests were beginning to talk, he pushed his face close to hers and whispered, "Follow me." She had no choice but to run after him, her hands still locked over her mouth in case the awful sound billowed forth again.

He did not stop until they had left the vicinity of the ballroom and entered a long, dark corridor that the little mermaid recognised as the hallway to the Prince's old chambers. He turned to her and took a hold of her wrists, forcing her arms down by her sides. Her skin seared at his touch.

"You can speak!" he declared. "Why did you pretend otherwise?"

But the little mermaid shook her head and tried to form the words, and nothing came out but a pitiful, gagging sound.

"I warn you, I am not to be trifled with!" said the Prince severely. "Are you trying to make a fool of me?" Indeed, he was angry. But perhaps this anger had less to do with being tricked and more to do with the fact that he had felt something unusual for this girl, and now his pride was hurt.

No! mouthed the little mermaid, and suddenly her vision became blurred and her eyes began to sting. The Prince instantly softened.

"Don't cry," he said, "don't cry." The little mermaid did not know what *cry* meant, but she was relieved by his quieter tones. "How can you laugh like that when you cannot speak? It is impossible."

And he took her face in his hands as if examining a sea-specimen, or even the head of his little black dog, and her mouth slowly parted. The creature within her chest began to beat heavily, and burn with a slow fire as the Prince inserted his finger inside of her mouth, and ran it along the jagged ridges of her teeth. She opened her mouth wider as he tilted her head toward the light, as his fingertip explored the bottom cavern of her jaw.

"Hmm," he said seriously, and released her. "It seems you have no tongue. It's very odd. But it's so dark out here and I am no expert. I insist you see a physician at your first convenience."

Before the little mermaid could wonder what a physician was, they were interrupted by the sound of discreet coughing behind them.

"Uncle!" stammered the Prince, and he jumped back from the girl as if she were contagious.

The King's brother chuckled and approached them, and the little mermaid instantly began to wonder if she had done something wrong. "At your ease, my boy," said the Uncle, "and who is this young lady?" And he looked at the mermaid as if he had forgotten entirely who she was.

"Funny you should ask that," began the Prince, "because I've been wondering myself."

The Uncle peered at her closer, and the little mermaid was frightened of the great animal on his face, and drew back.

"I don't think she likes you much, Uncle," commented the Prince dryly.

"No, indeed," agreed the King's brother, but he did not look at all angry. "I think I know this one. No, not in *that way*, thank you very much! I believe she is the nameless one, a foundling, if you will."

"She is an orphan, like me," said the Prince, and looked at the girl sadly. "She's a mute too, you know."

"Ah, but she is not deaf. It may seem rather rude

to mention her disability as if she were not standing among us."

"I meant no offence," said the Prince softly, and gave the mermaid a stiff little bow.

"I think the real question is," said the Uncle, crossing his arms over his chest in a businesslike way, "what are you going to do with her?"

The Prince looked at the girl, shivering at the unexpected attention, her hair in tangles and wearing the plainest dress imaginable. She seemed so frightened and forlorn that he saw himself in her place. He looked at her hard. He tried to see through her thoughts, through her pale skin and into her heart, but all he could find were images of himself. As he gazed at her with intensity, he could see a little boy marching solemnly down the city streets at his own mother's funeral procession. He saw tear-drenched coal-black eyes watching precisely where the snake-handled dagger sliced flesh. There was dark water and a constricting sensation of lungs. There was breathlessness. And finally, there were legless women and the air smelled of oranges.

"I believe I shall make her my companion," he declared.

TWELVE
THE MANY ADVANTAGES
OF A PERSONAL MAID

THE RAYS OF the sun warmed her skin as she lay in bed, toes curling in anticipation. She thought about the God and how much he had wanted her here and how right she was to trust her instinct. She felt exceedingly grateful, although she had known all along that the Prince would fall in love with her. It was impossible for it to be otherwise. Didn't she haul his drowning body miles in black water, her own strength siphoned into his body? Didn't she stroke the planes of his skin, and he looked right at her? Wasn't it meant to be from the moment she had first surfaced and seen him, lying on the bed of his sea-level chamber, lights glinting like water on his face?

She had always known it was the only outcome. It was

a matter of science, really. A matter of addition. Action plus action equals result.

She pressed her hands to her chest and wondered what it would feel like to finally have an Immortal Soul, that cherished golden drop of eternity, flutter within her. She had heard that there was a place where worshippers regularly went to meet God, a place where there were words and music and kneeling and singing. Perhaps this place could give her more insight into the mystery. However, she had heard that there was a ritual consuming of someone's flesh and blood, and that reminded her of the seawitch, and she was frightened. Perhaps it was a misunderstanding. Either way, nobody in the palace seemed terribly enthusiastic about it all, or had anything remarkable to say about the matter. She could not understand why humans were so blasé about their maker.

Sunlight bathed her new quarters and she looked around with pleasure. Her bed was an enormous, four-poster affair with all manner of pillows and quilts lodged into materials so soft they felt like the inside of thighs. There were enormous windows that stretched from the floor to the ceiling, where all she could see was ocean. There were chandeliers and heavy mahogany furnishings. There were carpets so thick that feet could sink up to the ankle.

And the wardrobe was a sight to behold. When the royal servants were sent to the upper housekeeping quarters to fetch her belongings, they had returned empty-handed. They reported that there was nothing worth bringing back, and somehow, a trove of gowns were fetched from nowhere and carried up numerous floors.

And here they were, perched inside the enormous wardrobe and winking at her with their seductive finery. The mermaid wondered how on earth she was to scrub bathroom tiles with all that on.

There was a discreet rap on her door and in came a young maid bearing a tray of breakfast. The little mermaid took that as a queue that she were running late, and scrambled out of bed. No matter how soft the carpet was, she felt she was treading on a bed of knives.

"Oh, no, no, no," chided the maid softly. "My lady should return to bed. Go on, lie back down. There's no need to be up and about on my account." And she giggled nervously and placed the tray on the bed.

"Eat up, then. There's toast and porridge and coffee from Spain." The little mermaid glanced at her own exotic aquarium in the corner of the room and thought privately that its inhabitants would make a much tastier breakfast.

"See that yellow stuff? It's called marmalade. It's made from oranges. It's the Prince's favourite, you see."

The little mermaid peered at the gelatinous substance with a new appreciation. She motioned for the girl to sit down, but the maid refused.

"None of that anymore, miss. You're one of *them* now. I've heard all about you, you know. That you were a servant like me, and not even a royal servant at that! And you caught the Prince's eye and now you're to live like a queen. It's like a fairy tale, isn't it?" And she leaned over and poured the aromatic coffee from the pitcher into a cup.

"What I wouldn't give to trade places with you. You're the first, you know. The Prince – I'm going to speak plainly, as you and I are from the same stock in the end – well, there were rumours for years that he didn't like women. That he was interested in...other boys, you know?" She smiled now, and her voice became loud again. "By God, he's handsome. Eh, you're a lucky one. But don't you worry about me. I'm as loyal as they come. And I've got an eye for his Uncle, you know. Oh, don't look so surprised! There's not a woman in this palace that don't." The mermaid understood the gist of this, and wondered why anyone would so much as look at the Uncle when the Prince was about. She could not understand what was so attractive about a man with a parasite on his face.

The maid, however, only noticed that the little mermaid had not begun to eat, so she reached down and buttered the toast for her. "By any means," she said, winking slyly, "I'd be interested to know how *it* was. I've always wondered how a prince would do *it*." The little mermaid did not know the meaning of "*it*", but if she had her voice back, she wouldn't have hesitated to declare that she had no intention of doing *it* with the Prince, and neither did she want to know what *it* meant. The way the serving girl was grinning was so vulgar, *it* was sure to be something very shocking indeed. That was the problem with these humans, they were altogether *scandalous*.

"I'm your Personal Maid, by the way. I'm specially trained. I know how to dress hair and select jewellery and what fabric goes with what occasion. I won't steer you wrong. And I want to be your friend, too. That is, if you like." The maid coloured prettily. "You can ask me anything you want, and I won't be telling nobody nothing! It's my special attribute, you see. I keep secrets."

The little mermaid smiled at the girl, who turned

bright red. "Not that you *can* ask me anything with your condition. I shouldn't have said that. Sometimes I talk too much. I'm sorry." But the little mermaid did not seem to mind at all, and the maid felt more at ease. "Well, eat up then. It'll be going cold. I'll be back later to dress you." And she tumbled out of the room.

After she had eaten what she could from the tray (plus several sea-snails and two fat anemone-fish from the aquarium) she was just wondering what Useful Occupation she'd have to employ now, when her Personal Maid bustled back in, breathless with excitement.

"Well, don't just lie there," reprimanded the girl, "for he's asking for you and wants to walk with you in the gardens. Get up! Get up! Oh, look at your hair, you're not fit to be seen!"

And the little mermaid was filled with gladness as the Personal Maid blustered her into a bathtub, wrenched a brush through the mass of hair, twisted and poked at it until her scalp ached, and bullied her into the tightest, shiniest, most elaborate and most unnecessary garment she'd ever seen. When she finally beheld her own reflection in the looking-glass, she gasped. For the woman standing before her was not herself. It was not the little mermaid who asked too many questions, nor was it the housekeeping servant with blood in her shoes. She did not know who this woman was.

After the Personal Maid had given her several confusing directions to the upper courtyard, the little mermaid set off. She shuffled down her own corridor, in the royal wing of the palace, and wondered exactly which doors belonged to the Prince. As she roamed the hallways, several lords and ladies of the court greeted her as they went by, and after a time, the mermaid felt it best to merely smile and nod. Several times she nearly tripped on layers and layers of skirt, and the high heels caused her feet pain like never before.

But all the bother and inconvenience fled her as she approached the courtyard and the Prince turned around, his eyes lighted upon her. Several functions of her body ceased working at once.

"You look unrecognisable," said the Prince finally, as he took her hands in his. "I'd never have known you." He turned to his Uncle, who she'd only just noticed, standing beside him. "Is all this necessary, do you think?"

"Only if you don't want tongues wagging further," said the Uncle dryly. "We can't have your companion running about in rags, she'd be unfit to be seen." His tone was harsher than usual. His gaze swept the little mermaid from head to toe and he omitted a gruff sound, turned on his heel and left.

"Never mind him," assured the Prince. "I don't care a bit what people say. Is this not my palace? Are they not my subjects? I wish to do what I please, and I wish that you would too. Come, let me show you something."

He held out his hand and the little mermaid took it. There was a little-used stairwell in the back tower of the palace and the Prince led her down, floors and floors of backache and tripping and feet feeling like their bones were on the verge of snapping. Finally, they ventured through a small wooden door and there they were, standing on the edge of a magnificent orange grove. A cloying scent filled the air.

"It's wonderful, isn't it?" said the Prince. And his eyes took in every tree and every blossom. The little mermaid watched his face and agreed that it was wonderful.

He began to examine the nearest tree for ripe fruit and called over his shoulder, "You can take your shoes off, if you like. I see how much pain you're in. Why women wear such awkward things is beyond me."

The little mermaid reached down and painstakingly took off one shoe, and the other. She noticed that her toes were already stained brown and sticky. As the Prince threw her a round, perfect orange which fell into her lap, he noticed her feet as well and grimaced. He picked up her shoes and examined them, and before the little mermaid could stop him, he had hurled both over the garden wall. Satisfied with himself, he smirked. "And never let me see you wear such shoes again."

The little mermaid was delighted and nodded enthusiastically. She began to examine the orange, eager to please. "You have to peel it, like this," said the Prince, and he took the fruit from her and began to peel and quarter it. "Taste it," he commanded. She did not need to be told twice.

Instantly, her eyes welled up with fluid, for the fruit filled ever corner of her mouth with a sour, rancid taste. Its texture was like old animal flesh, and it bubbled with fetid acid on her tongue. When she could stand it no longer, she spat it unceremoniously at the Prince's feet.

His eyes were wide with surprise. He ate some himself to see if it were bad, but it was sweet and rich and perfect. "Strange girl," he commented, "you have very odd tastes." And he got to his feet in one fluid movement and left her there.

The little mermaid did not follow him but watched as he wandered about the grove, stroking the bare white bodies of the trees as if they were the breasts of a well-endowed woman, he an elderly man in his last days of physical delights. He seemed to forget all about her as he walked, lost in his thoughts.

At last he returned, and looked at her without pleasure. "I will see you back," he said gruffly. He helped her to her feet but did not meet her eyes. Together they ascended the tower steps, this time the Prince striding before her as if he could not wait to be rid of her, the mermaid struggling with every step she took. He walked down the hall in a biting, hurried pace and stopped abruptly before her door.

"I do not require your companionship for the rest of the day," he said brusquely. He held the door open for her.

Confused and disappointed, she brushed past him to reach the inside of her sanctuary. She turned her face away to avoid her nose from touching his, so close was their proximity. Before she could take another step he murmured softly, "Allow me." To her very great surprise, he smudged the paint off her eyelids and cheeks with the palm of his free hand. Her body broke out in goose pimples as he wiped away the scarlet lip colour her maid had been so insistent upon. "I don't wish to see this again," he said softly. "Will you promise me?"

Yes, mouthed the little mermaid. The Prince gave her a twisted smile, and then he was gone.

The rest of the evening was spent in silent uproar. She frantically whipped through the pages of her memory to gain the reason why she had so displeased the Prince. It could not have been the oranges, for he was surely testing her by presenting her with such a foul food. Surely it had been poison. Then why did he then taste some himself? Human customs, she decided, were not sound-minded.

It dawned on her that she knew little about her Prince, and he about her. She searched her mind for a way to convey to him more about herself and what she had done for him, but she did not know how. For the first time, she regretted giving her tongue in payment for the witch's brew. She should have negotiated with her. Rumours said that the sea-witch was fond of a good bargain.

She went to her dresser and searched it thoroughly. She emptied every jar of powder, paint and rouge into her washbasin. She added the vials of perfume, and threw the hairpins in too for good measure. In a sort of frantic fury, her next destination was the wardrobe, where she carefully examined every garment, angrily tearing the most ornamental and beautiful off their hooks and into the carpet. Her eyes began to sting, but she did not know why.

Her angry reverie was interrupted as her Personal Maid entered, bearing yet another tray of food. "They are dining in the grand hall, so my question is, what are you doing here? Are you the Prince's companion or aren't you?"

The mermaid looked up from where she lay in a messy puddle in the middle of the floor. She looked at her maid mournfully.

"There, there," said the Personal Maid. "I'm sure he will invite you tomorrow."

But the little mermaid would not hear it, shaking her head savagely. The maid was astonished. "And why ever wouldn't he? Eh, you haven't done something to offend his Majesty, have you?"

She shook her head again and gestured with her arms wildly. "Ah," said the maid, "you don't know. Well," she said practically, "you've made a real mess of this room in your little tantrum. But I'll set things right while you eat. And you had better eat this time," she warned with narrowed eyes, "unlike your shenanigans with breakfast."

Later, after the mermaid had dined, not unpleasantly, on broiled fish, her Personal Maid dressed her in a soft nightgown and tucked her into bed. She made sure the table lamps were lit, and checking that the door was locked, sat on the edge of the bed and gazed at the girl as if she were a very difficult project indeed.

"So he didn't like your appearance today," she said, "it's not the end of the world. Don't look so surprised. I wasn't spying or nothing. But I wasn't born yesterday, and a wash basin full of cosmetics could only mean one thing."

The little mermaid nodded forlornly, glad to finally have a confidante, someone who understood, even if she understood little.

"You know what I gather? I reckon you're like a child in a grown-up's body. You don't know much about men and women, and you certainly don't know a whole lot about *it*. Haven't you ever been with a man?"

The little mermaid shook her head, wondering how to express that the Prince was the first man she'd ever seen, let alone was with.

And the Personal Maid, with her silly head and her heart of gold, leaned toward the mermaid and shared her wealth of information about men, bodies, tastes, lies, tricks and sex. The mermaid understood more than she expected, and with her eyes wide and her mouth even wider, she dissected the information and stored it away in her book of humanity.

It took a long time to fall asleep that night, for she had realised that there was far more to men and women than love and weddings and the impartation of the Immortal Soul. It was a deep well of mystery and she had barely scratched the surface.

Thirteen

THE PHYSICIAN'S VERDICT

DESPITE HER EARLIER assumptions that the Prince would have nothing more to do with her, there was a message in the morning informing her to stay in her chambers, for a physician was coming to examine her. Although the little mermaid knew exactly why she could not speak, and that the whole affair was completely unnecessary, she held hope in the fact that the Prince had added a postscript asking her to meet him in the library afterwards.

The physician had come and gone, a rather uncomfortable situation that included a lot of poking about with metal instruments and muttering under his breath. He had looked upon the mermaid like she was a simpleton, and made a great deal of comments about the oddity of her dental structure.

"Why," he had spluttered, "it's like you'd spent your whole life chewing fish bones!"

True to her word, the Personal Maid dressed her charge in the plainest, least elaborate gown that she could muster from the fine wardrobe, and did not re-introduce cosmetics into their repertoire. She brushed out the mermaid's hair and let it hang down her back, and sent her on her way without so much as a spritz of rose water.

The Prince barely looked up when she entered the library. To say it was like any other ordinary library would be a lie. It was a book mausoleum, a dark, cold hall of marble that housed thousands of volumes to be consumed not on thick, fluffy sofas, but at hard concrete tables. It encouraged the serious scholar and not the pleasure-seeking reader.

"Come here," he said in commanding tones. "Sit by me." The mermaid timidly did so, and as she sat at his left elbow, she noticed that he smelled of grass and paper and something smoky. "You can read, can't you?"

Now one thing that she had learned from her Personal Maid in their illuminating discussion was that it never hurt to lie to the one you love. So she nodded enthusiastically. "Excellent," said the Prince, although he did not look as if he found anything excellent this morning. He eyed the little mermaid studiously, but made no comment about her appearance.

He turned away from her and continued reading an enormous volume. The little mermaid rose and ran her fingers lightly over the spines of books in nearest shelves of books before she selected one. It was full of alien markings, so cramped and confusing that it gave her a headache to look at it. But at least there were pictures, albeit strange ones of circles and lines and little else. She examined them carefully.

"See here," interrupted the Prince suddenly, "this author is full of contradictions! Here he is saying one thing, and now he changes his mind! He is denying his very thesis!" He began to read aloud from several passages, during which the little mermaid closed her book on her lap and watched his lips as he spoke. She understood something about a canal, and a bit about uncivilised people living somewhere in large groups. "*Water Resources in Southern America*," mocked the Prince. "If my father had used these methods, we would have dried this kingdom out long ago." And with as much careless abandon as he demonstrated with the shoes, he pitched the volume over his shoulder. Believing this to be some sort of ritual, the mermaid quite happily did the same with hers.

The Prince looked amused, if not a little surprised. "And what did that book do to offend you so?" he asked, craning his head to see the cover of the volume from where it had landed, spread-eagled, on the ground.

"*Pythagorus' Theorem*," he read aloud. "Perhaps your tastes are not so strange after all." And his face opened up like the sky after a day of sleet, and he smiled.

The rest of the day continued in a similar fashion, the little mermaid pretending to read whilst secretly observing the Prince under lowered eyelids, and the Prince interrupting frequently to read aloud or make a comment. The time ticked by rapidly, for the little mermaid never tired of looking at her companion, as every moment revealed a new shadow or detail. Like how there were several course dark hairs connected to the regal sweep of his brows. And how the ball of his throat bobbed up and down like an apple in water every time he swallowed.

The Prince, on the other hand, enjoyed the girl's company, for there was something about her presence that calmed him. It wasn't that she was mute, for several times already he had guessed correctly what she was trying to communicate. Her facial expressions, he found, were accurate and easily read. There was no guile or artifice hidden behind her eyes. She was an excellent listener, too. Her attention was focussed entirely upon him when he spoke, and her gaze did not flitter off here or there as if she were growing bored, or thinking of other things. Neither did it hurt that she was nice to look at.

It did not occur to him to probe his new companion for her history. He was not the sort of infuriating lover one sees on a daily basis, who milks his partner relentlessly for useless background information. The type that wants to know all the intimacies of their beloved's childhood, every small, miniscule inclination, and how many lovers they've previously had. There was no misguided satisfaction to be found in that, and the Prince was practical, if not unimaginative. He understood that the girl could not speak, incapable of telling him her own name, let alone chapters of her past. He did not wonder about her family or origins. All her cared to know was that she was pleasing, and she was here for however long he wished her to be.

He was so gratified with her behaviour in the library

that he decided he may as well invite her to dinner. As she took her leave of him, radiant with delight, to make ready for the evening, he returned to his book. But he found he could not concentrate. There were two faces in his head and they were beginning to merge into one another, to make a whole new, unfamiliar face. It frightened him.

When the mermaid had finally located the royal dining room, a visually stunning hall adorned with French windows that invited the view of the sea on the left side and the mountains on the right, she was greeted first by the tantalising aroma of exotic dishes. There were at least twenty of them, all set out down the length of the table in single file. They were covered with silver lids, the reflections of the candlelight burning within them. When she had inhaled the spectacle, she noticed that someone was sitting at the foot of the table, in the semi-darkness. She approached him with anticipation.

She could see his broad shoulders now, covered by a heavy velvet cloak. The light moved and she could see his eyes, piercing and thrilling and watching her every move like a hawk watches prey. She could see the curls that fell against his forehead. As she drew close enough, the candlelight flooded him entirely. But she sucked in her breath sharply when she saw the large, frightening animal upon his face.

Diverting her eyes, she fumbled for the nearest chair, and threw herself upon it. What was she thinking? Was she so in love that she thought every man was her Prince? And now she'd made a fool of herself in front of *him*. Her cheeks burned scarlet, for she had just endured her first brush with shame. She was aware now of the sounds of breathing all around her, and realised she had failed to notice the presence of the servants, watching and waiting, in the dark sleeves of the hall. She coloured further, determined to keep her eyes on her plate until something came along to rescue her.

"Am I that bad?" drifted his voice across the table.

The little mermaid continued to gaze at her plate but shook her head in response.

"Do I frighten you?" he continued.

She shook her head furiously, although she could not account for the hairs on the back of her neck standing up and clinging to the static in the air.

"There is no need to lie to me," he said. "I have no intention of harming you."

And it occurred to her then that his voice was like the golden stuff her Personal Maid spread her toast with, the substance made by those little black-and-yellow flying creatures.

"Won't you look at me?"

The creature in the little mermaid's chest thudded, and she was sure the invisible servants could hear it too.

"Please?"

Slowly, she lifted her gaze off the table to meet his eyes. Something akin to a lighted fuse of dynamite seared through her. They stared at each other for a long moment, long enough for the two serving girls in the back to nudge each other and wink.

"Sorry I'm late," came a voice behind them, "urgent business." Instantly, the spell was broken as the Prince strode into the hall, falling elegantly into the chair opposite the little mermaid. "I'm starved. Uncle, you should have gone ahead without me."

"No meal is to go ahead without the presence of His Majesty," replied the Uncle.

The Prince ceremoniously lifted the lid off the nearest dish, and the feast began. The little mermaid busied herself with studying the food, for she did not want to meet his eyes again, nor the Prince's, for that matter. She did not know why.

She was pleased to note that the menu tonight was an array of sea-food, from stuffed octopus to steaming, aromatic lobster. With a comforting sense of familiarity, she nodded to the staff who appeared at her elbow serving portions of food. After her experiences in the palace, she was proficient with cutlery and other such utensils, and used most with skill. The Prince watched with amusement as she ate without common restraint.

"A most unusual find," commented the Uncle quietly, as their companion was too engrossed in her meal to notice anything else.

"Yes," said the Prince absent-mindedly. "I see there is no meat tonight."

"I thought we agreed that I would arrange the menu three times a week."

"Yes, but still there is no meat and I like meat."

"Well, why don't you order all week, then?"

"Because I don't want to," responded the Prince.

"This is why the palace needs a lady in charge," said the Uncle tellingly. There was a silence before the Uncle gently inquired, "What urgent business?"

"Hmmm?" The Prince busied himself trying to slide seeds out of a tomato with his fork.

"Why you were late. The urgent business."

"Oh," said the Prince, making a great show of examining a successfully emancipated seed, "Just that thing... I've mentioned it...been a busy week..." And his voice trailed into silence as he popped the entire tomato into his mouth.

The Uncle frowned at his nephew and was only distracted when the little mermaid, quite full, exhaled a loud, satisfied sigh and fell back into her chair. This brought smiles from both gentleman, and there was small talk, and a little banter about the weather and the palace's entertainment schedule for the week.

After the men had eaten their fill and engaged the little mermaid in light conversation, the Uncle pulled back his chair and stood to leave.

"I'll join you in your chamber to go over figures from the treasury," said the Prince.

"Please don't," replied the Uncle slyly, "for I'll have no one disturbing me in my chambers tonight." And to the mermaid's very great shock, he turned towards her and winked rakishly. Then he strode from the room without another word.

"My Uncle," said the Prince by way of an excuse, "his behaviour...that is to say, his conduct...he hasn't been the same since the war."

The little mermaid nodded, for she had detected the shadows in his Uncle's eyes, and sometimes she saw figures there, black figures with their hair on fire. During her housekeeping days, she had even seen a ghost in the hallway, and it had kissed the Uncle gently and he had followed it out of sight.

"I was wondering if you might like to see the stables? We have some new thoroughbreds in from Spain – do you like horses?"

And there he was, by her side. He took her hand in his, and just like the old castle ghosts, led her to another world.

The court had mixed opinions about the girl. The women, old or young, married or not married yet, all held a bitter grudge because they had not been chosen. They talked incessantly amongst themselves of what they considered to be the mermaid's flaws. The way she dressed, for instance. Her disability. How she considered herself too beautiful for cosmetics. That infuriatingly arrogant inclination of the head when she passed by. How the Prince always searched a room for her. How his eyes became alive when she made her way toward him.

The men, on the other hand, had only praise for the Prince's companion. Here was a woman who knew when to hold her tongue. And secretly, they were all a little relieved at the proof that the Prince was not inclined towards men. They had forgotten, with all their money and meetings and distractions, that even a man-lover has certain tastes, and a specimen of the male gender was not enough to simply satisfy.

The common conception was that the Prince intended to marry the girl. Half the court was relieved, for it was well-known that he had had a difficult life, and they loved their monarch and wanted to allow him one small happiness. Half were indignant - the older ones, the ones with old money turning their blood black - who wanted a royal marriage. They did not think a dumb foundling, with no background or family connections, would make a very good queen at all. They would pester the Uncle about it on many a social occasion, but he would smile blandly and direct the conversation elsewhere. They did not dare mention it to the Prince himself.

The little mermaid was oblivious to the minefield of gossip she had ignited, for no person really existed but the Prince. (True, her Personal Maid was like the sun orbiting around her life and the Uncle skirted throughout her days like the shadow of some unpleasant thing.) She was mindful of the fact that the Prince warmed to her more and more each day, slowly drawing close on morning strolls in the courtyard and sessions in the library that would last until midnight. She realised he trusted her completely on the day her door opened a fraction and little black creature had tumbled in, delighting her with its funny expression and the gambolling of its small legs. She fed it morsels from her breakfast tray and it had urinated on the carpet.

The Prince's affection could be easily measured by the amount and length of his smiles, and the potency of his gaze as it occasionally smouldered upon her, when he thought no one was looking. He would take her to several private and secret corners of the palace, balconies sprinkled with remnants of gargoyle-protectors, tower turrets coated in cobwebs, spiders leering at them and rubbing their legs together in anticipation. But they never returned to the orange grove, and he did not take her outside the palace walls.

Every Tuesday the Personal Maid would appear with a bunch of assorted, mismatched wildflowers lying on the tea tray. "From His Lordship," she would say, and place them in an ornate vase on the night stand. When she left, the little mermaid would take them from the vase, their stems dripping water, and place them in the mouth-wash glass.

It was times like these that the little mermaid could clearly see the parallels between herself and the Prince. She wondered if he too had seen them and when the light would flare in his eyes.

"I've never left the kingdom before," the Prince had said only yesterday, during one of their intimate dinners where the Uncle had excuse to dine elsewhere. "I used to dream of running away. Stowing away in a farmer's hay wagon. Hiring myself out to a quiet little farm and looking after the pigs."

The little mermaid looked at the Prince knowingly, and he dropped his head. "Well," he faltered, "I did leave the kingdom once, actually. It was an…accident." And his gaze trailed off to the left, and he watched as the night-mist settled over the seas.

"Have you ever felt sad? Not sad for an instant, or sad for a day. A kind of sadness you can only be born with. It covers you like a blanket. It follows you like the smell of garlic. And you do…things…to help you forget."

The mermaid nodded her head solemnly. In her mind's eye she could see the snake-handled dagger.

"I was sad once. But now, things are changing. Now I have you. I must tell you what it is I so admire about you. It's not your beauty, although my Uncle seems to think so." At this, the Prince smiled, and the little mermaid's eyes grew round with anticipation. "It's that I trust you. You aren't like other women. You won't sneak into my treasury and steal my gold. You won't slip into my bed at night and secret a child out of me." At this thought, he grinned. "I've never had a friend before. If I had a problem, I think you would be there. If I were drowning, I think you would save me."

At this, the little mermaid jumped in her seat. Forgetting herself, she grasped the Prince's hand and squeezed it, for she jubilantly believed he had finally remembered who she was. But the Prince laughed and lightly disengaged his hand. "I'm giving you a compliment," he explained, "and there's no need to thank me."

One night, the Uncle threw a banquet for the arrival of some ambassador from one distant land or another. The Prince attended the feast with the mermaid on his arm, and after he had made a fine speech, he was seated at the head of the table with her on his right. He did not pay the little mermaid more attention that usual, but rather he spoke to all his guests in an intelligent and amiable manner. All she was required to do was smile, nod and flitter from person to person as if shackled to his side. Once, when she was engaged in conversation with a kind-hearted, elderly lord, she felt the hand of the Prince on her back. Instantly, she withdrew from the one-sided discussion, and in a cocoon that protected them both from the laughter, boasting, scrapings and music, he whispered, "You look beautiful tonight." Her cheeks were scarlet for the rest of the evening.

Later, the guests moved into the nearest ballroom, for the ambassador's wife had mentioned that she was inclined to dance that very evening. The musicians carried their violas and cellos up several flights of stairs and assembled in a corner, striking a waltz. The servants bustled about, moving chairs and tables and candelabras, but nobody noticed them. The Prince and the little mermaid watched the couples dance. They looked so enchanting as their bodies moved fluidly to the music. The men were entranced by their ladies, and there was not a single woman who wasn't laughing.

Suddenly, the mermaid forgot that he was the head of the entire kingdom, and the lord of her whole world. She forgot that he was the reason for her pain and struggles. She forgot his weight and importance, his frowns and disinclinations. However, she did recall that she was still a princess, and that her father was the king of an entire realm. And she reached for his hands and pulled him toward the dance floor.

And so the court beheld their Prince dancing for the first time of his life. He allowed himself to be led across the room, for the mermaid knew music and she knew the power of her body, although her feet ached and her shoes filled gradually with blood. She was entwined in his arms, her body brushed against his, and sometimes he felt the sting of her hair as it whipped across his cheek. Possession crept into his fingers as he grasped her waist tighter, and he kept his eyes on her face. Every thought, every plan made in the night, escaped him for those brief moments.

They danced together the whole night, and the Prince felt several things happen at once. He felt like he was drunk, for he was giddy and could barely keep his balance. Unplanned words leaked from his mouth that he could not stop. The muscles burned in his body and music played in his head and his groin tingled unmercifully. He breathed in the air and it somehow tasted different. He forgot the burden his father left to him and was ignorant to the discerning stare of his Uncle as he ushered his companion from the ballroom.

He walked her to her room more slowly than usual, for he realised that what transpired this night could not possibly be captured again. The palace was bathed with the hues of bruises in the half-moon light. The statues created shadows that were almost human and every stair creaked, and every object whispered something – advice, suggestions, caution. They returned to her room in silence and stood at the door, waiting for the other to move.

"The physician told me," began the Prince after a very long time, "that your tongue had been severed with a knife or a weapon."

The little mermaid began to nod slowly.

"It is true then," said the Prince darkly, and his features blackened. "Who did this to you?"

She sighed and shrugged her shoulders like it did not matter.

"What an ordeal to have gone through," he murmured, and his body drew closer to hers, and his fingers timidly touched her jaw. "Let me see."

The little mermaid motioned that it was too dark and too futile. But the Prince was determined and morbidly curious and once again his fingers found his way into her mouth like some demented dentist, and she opened wide, ever the obedient patient.

"I can't see anything," said the Prince after a while. He removed his hand abruptly and stared down at her. "Poor thing." But he did not withdraw his nearness and his hand fell onto her forearm. He grasped it.

Before he realised what he was doing, he lowered his face toward hers. His curls brushed against her forehead and the tip of his nose skimmed hers. His breath enveloped her senses for it was ragged, shredded. His grip on her arm tightened and he kissed her. It was tentative, like the launching of a first ship, or the blind newborn minks emerging from a hole into the searing light of day. Instinct invaded and it became a stained shattering of taste and sensation, of blood, of knives and their blades. And everywhere, all around them, in their nostrils and in their pores, bled the scent of oranges.

When at last they broke apart, the Prince looked down at her. She was flushed and startled and inanely happy. He felt his conscience grip him and begin to tug him away. To conceal what he believed to be a visible struggle, he said rather stupidly, "Your heart is beating so fast."

Her hands flew to her chest, and found the creature thumping away, desperate to escape. Her heart. So she had a heart after all. Thoughts flew through her mind, images of her nanny and the dead heart she claimed all merfolk possessed. She recalled the first time she knew she was different, when she was just a child and suspected that her own beatless heart was malfunctioning, and she had begun to hide her emotions. How quiet the chambers of the underwater palace were, until she entered them. She was reminded of the sea-witch as she vomited her own Immortal Soul. The sea-witch with her own heart like a relentless, forbidding drum. And finally, she remembered an image of broken glass and black hair so old that sea-lice had half eaten it away.

But these recollections that should have been stitched together with bone and used as armour to protect her and prevent what happened next, she discarded like soiled napkins. For there was her Prince, and he had held her in his arms, and he had swept his tongue into the cavern of her mouth, and she tasted the champagne and olives of his mouth, and it tasted like dizziness.

When she entered her chamber alone, she sat down in a pile of contentment and gazed out the window at the sea. There, over the dark horizon, came a formidable shape. As it drew closer and her eyes adjusted, she realised that it was the form of someone she had known once. It was the Sea King himself, staring up at her. She flew to the window and in the human custom, waved her arm frantically. The Sea King slowly raised one hand in the air. She believed then that it was in greeting.

FOURTEEN
SICKENINGLY SALTY

WHEN THE PERSONAL Maid entered her chamber the next morning, the little mermaid was already up and dressed. She could barely contain her excitement for the day ahead. Having lain there for half the night reliving every sensation, tasting his mouth and the pressure of his lips against hers, she was bleary-eyed and fatigued. Desperately, she needed it to happen again. She made half-formed plans to perform the act just as soon as she saw him again.

Starving, she wolfed down the tea and toast. The Personal Maid gazed at her suspiciously. "Eh now, what's got into you?" she asked, pouring another cup of tea. "You like the cat what got the cream!"

The little mermaid turned to her maid, eyes shining, and grinned. She brought her fingertips to her lips and pressed down on them, in gesture.

Gasping, the Personal Maid squealed, "He kissed you?"

The mermaid's eyebrows flew up, for she did not know this word. "Kiss!" explained the maid, and she kissed her own fingertips with gusto, and placed them over the mermaid's mouth gently. "That's kiss."

The little mermaid nearly laughed as she nodded enthusiastically. "Well done," said the maid proudly, "do you think he'll marry you?"

She nodded and grinned and threw her arms into the air in pure happiness. After all this time, the loss of her voice, the blood that seeped from the ball of her feet, the God had saw fit to grant her wishes. She was marrying the man she loved. She was getting an Immortal Soul. The sea-witch and all her scepticism was defeated.

"Congratulations," breathed the Personal Maid. "I'm ever so happy for you." She smiled and hummed as she took the empty breakfast tray away.

The little mermaid settled herself comfortably on a couch to await the Prince's summons. The morning passed slowly, but he did not come. After the maid had been and gone with the lunch tray, he still had not come. She contemplated leaving the room to search for him, but thought it might appear too eager. She created excuses for him – urgent meetings and council queries – after all, he was the ruler of a realm. She tried to recall how busy her own father had always been. Finally, her heart lurched as there was a drumming at the door. She hastened to her feet, ran to it and flung it open, beaming.

It was not the Prince. It was his Uncle, dressed in a stately manner, with that dark and hideous animal clawing to his face. She drew back instinctively, overcome with disappointment.

"His Majesty is presently engaged and cannot enjoy the pleasure of your company," he said stiffly. "He sent me to entertain you instead."

The little mermaid frowned at him in confusion.

"That is, if you consent. You may have better things to do with your time then spend it with a man you obviously find dull, and dare I say, frightening?" And he smiled at the girl, but she could barely make it out due to the density of the animal.

"I may not be young or dashing, but I've seen a few things in my time and am quite an excellent guide. I thought I might show you the kingdom. What do you say?"

His eyes twinkled and he leaned closer to the girl. "I am not going to hurt you. Believe me."

And suddenly, she did. After all, it would not do to insult the Prince's only living relative. Besides, perhaps she would learn more about her lover through him, perhaps droplets of knowledge would spill from the conversation. And she certainly was interested in seeing the rest of the human world.

So she bowed to him, as was the custom, and the Uncle took her arm and drew her away. Down flights of stairs they went, down past the portrait corridor of the kings of old, past treasure and armour and vestiges of royalty. The sun momentarily blinded them as they stepped foot outside, and the air was filled with the aroma of pines and salt. The mermaid had the sensation of cobwebs pulled away where they had congealed around her eyes.

Saddled into the sable mare that the Prince had taught her to ride, the Uncle and two servants began to canter. The heavy iron gates segregating the palace from the common world parted and they passed through. The King's brother led the troupe up and through the limestone cliffs on what had once been a dangerous trek, now fortified through the labours of many a stonemason and his Chinamen. There were many varieties of flying-fish, or *birds* as the humans liked to call them, that frequented the cliffs, sometimes daring to swoop down on them and bray their melancholy cries.

Upon their descent of the cliffs, the little mermaid beheld the city that lay in the valley behind the castle. It was a collage of colours and sights and sounds, all mismatched and sized differently, every shape and every scent. There were houses, some stately, with marble trimmings and prison-like fences, but mainly they were squat and modest, boasting nothing but a herb garden and a host of squawking chickens. The markets were indescribable, with squabbling people and the chink of heavy purses, fish scales floating in the air and dogs begging for a scrap. The little mermaid noticed with surprise that the citizens did not pay for their purchases with an ear or a finger or a braid of hair – indeed, all of the people seemed completely intact. Instead, they handed (or sometimes flung) heavy golden discs to each other, which they instantly pocketed. She was also amazed to see that some commoners were just as handsome or beautiful as the sires and madams of court. There were peasant girls, their ample bosoms heaving from pulling reluctant sows, who brushed excrement from their exquisite faces. There were young men too that sauntered in the corners, gazing up at the richer men who walked by, whispering temptations with their sensual lips, gazing beguilingly as dark lashes swept their angular cheek bones.

There was music, unrefined music played by boys with only one stocking on a large, hollow, six-stringed instrument that sat in their laps. It was lively, and people's feet tapped unconsciously as they heard it. And there seemed to be a complete absorption of love in the city, all kinds of love. There were young people so locked in embrace they appeared to be wrestling, fathers who swung their daughters in the air, sisters who held hands and pushed their heads together, whispering frothy secrets. But best of all were the elderly folk, so enmeshed in lifetimes of hard work their bodies seemed to be all right angles, who would look at their spouses with the eyes of the young, a whole story told in the brush of a shoulder. These people would all look up as they spied the royal emblem, and smile and wave and shout salutations as the troupe rode by. The little mermaid would try to shout back, her mouth forming silent words. Her arm soon ached from waving.

The Uncle proved to be an outstanding guide, and explained landmarks and behaviours with such simplicity and humour that the mermaid laughed aloud once or twice. Her horse fell into an easy pace beside his, and he often kept his eyes upon her, judging her reactions. She felt less nervous in his presence, and recalled the way he had come to her aid on her very first day, saving her from the wrath of the Lower Housekeeper. He was a difficult man, she decided, who knew how to make things easy.

As it began to grow dark and the group made to

ascend the cliffs once more, they passed a small concrete church that was used to being overlooked on account of its size and unimpressive features. But the little mermaid heard the faint chanting from the inside and elated, pulled her mare to a halt and slid out of the saddle. The Uncle and servants followed suit, and soon they were seated in the midst of worshippers, who knelt and fingered wooden necklaces, one bead at a time. They whispered many things and names she did not understand and for once, the Uncle did not explain.

There were a great many oddities in the church. There were statues of people, life-sized, especially of a beautiful lady holding a baby with a golden halo around its head. The queerest and most disturbing of all, thought the mermaid, were the stained glass pictures depicting the journey of a sad man who carried a cross of wood. There were pictures of him tortured and strung to the very cross he carried. In the final picture, he had left behind his grave and was flying up toward heaven. The creature inside the man's chest was exposed. It was red and thorns surrounded it. She wondered why there were no pictures of the God, the great fiery ball of heaven who bathed all things in its light.

She stole a glance at the Uncle, but he was not looking at her. Instead, he rested an elbow upon his knee and cupped his face in his hand, staring at the altar in a cold anger. The mermaid wondered why the altar did not split open from the potency of his gaze. She shivered, hoping she was never on the other side of that stare. He muttered something soft under his breath, like he was addressing an invisible person, and then snorted. He rearranged his legs and leaned back into the pew, crossing his arms firmly over his chest. The hairs on the mermaid's arms were standing on end, and they brushed against his sleeve.

There was a little man dressed in purple with the same cross around his neck. He read from a large book and said a great many things the mermaid did not understand. Suddenly, the choir began to sing and the congregation rose. The little mermaid listened intently and closed her eyes, and she was awash with pain and pleasure. Every hair on her body uncurled and stood flat and rigid. Her eyes stung beneath her eyelids like they had been doused in acid. Her heart was heavy yet light at the same time. A reassuring hand squeezed her knee through her dress and her eyes flew open. Through her blurred vision, she saw the face of the Uncle, who had not risen either, but had stayed seated beside her.

"We must go now," he whispered, "it is almost dark."

And obediently, the mermaid got to her feet. They exited the church as quietly as they could and mounted their horses. The little mermaid could not help but recall the man's face in the stained glass as he ascended to heaven. If he were no longer sad, why were there thorns around his heart?

Although she had enjoyed the outing, she missed the Prince terribly and so the next day, she waited eagerly for him. Finally, there came the anticipated knock at the door, but when the mermaid opened it, she saw it was the Uncle again. She could not hide her disappointment.

"He's left, I'm afraid," said the Uncle by way of greeting. The Personal Maid immediately diverted her eyes and busied herself tidying the closet. But the little mermaid had noticed and she glanced at her maid with suspicion.

When? she mouthed, wondering why the Prince had not told her the night he had so rapturously kissed her.

"Yesterday. He's gone on a journey. I can't say any more than that, I'm afraid, because even I do not know the details."

Despite her surprise, her busy mind began to calculate how long a journey was likely to take.

"But if you would care to meet me at the stables at noon, there is something I particularly wish to show you."

The little mermaid nodded absently and before the Uncle had time to excuse himself, had sunk into bed and drawn the covers over her head.

"I'm awfully sorry, miss," said the Personal Maid gently when the Uncle had left the room.

In response, the little mermaid flung off the blankets and stared at the maid fiercely.

"I wanted to tell you, really I did," the maid stammered, "but you were so happy yesterday and I didn't want nothing to ruin that."

The little mermaid sighed in exasperation and motioned with her hands wildly.

"Well, I did hear on the servant's grapevine that it was a very urgent and secret sort of journey. No one knows where to, or for how long. The Prince took three of his best men, from the army that is, and no supplies. And he left without telling a soul – he left his uncle a *note*."

The news did little to appease the mermaid, and to

make her sentiments quite clear, she flung a pillow at her maid and returned the covers over her head.

❧

Precious little did the journey to the ruins do to raise the girl's spirits. The Uncle kept a keen eye on her in the carriage, but she did not care to notice. She stared glumly out the window and looked at the scenery, scenery that anyone in their right mind would be enchanted by, without seeing it. He had tried, unsuccessfully, to distract her by regaling the history of the area several times. Sometimes her brow would furrow when a particularly dark thought crossed her mind, and her nostrils would exhume furious bursts of air. Other than that, the carriage was silent.

Finally, they had reached their destination and the mermaid was diverted from her musings by the sight of a long-corroded pier and what appeared to be a mountain of rubble at the end of it. She followed the Uncle out of the carriage and shut her door with more force than necessary.

The planks of the pier were rotted for the most part, so the Uncle took her elbow to guide her along. From the slits between the boards, the mermaid could make out thick slabs of concrete embedded in the ocean floor. She gasped when they came to the end of the pier, for the ruins were enormous, piles and piles of wreckage lay on top of the other, more than what seemed possible.

"Hundred of years ago," said the Uncle in his uncomfortably alluring voice, "before our kingdom was a great city, it was nothing but a small village of fisherman. These ruins are from the lighthouse, which served as a beacon for all ships, from Africa to the wild Nordic lands. It was said to be the greatest lighthouse ever built, but why it was built here, in a shanty village of no consequence, no one ever knew. But one day, despite its quality foundations and years of reliability, it just collapsed."

The Uncle squatted down and took a piece of the ancient rubble in his hand and examined it. "There are plenty of myths surrounding this place," he continued. "Some say they hear the cries of the very building coming up from within these stones. They say that the ruins are mourning. Still others say they sometimes see the ghost of a woman, a beautiful woman who once may have lived here, searching desperately through the rubble. The ghost searches until her fingers are bleeding grey, phantom blood. But she never finds what she is looking for." With one steady motion, he pitched the debris he held right out to sea.

"I brought you here to tell you this: sometimes what we are searching for does not exist. We may sacrifice for it, even bleed for it, but it was never meant to be ours." He drew closer to the little mermaid and she shivered, although it was not cold. "Even the strongest things, things we rely on the most, things we believe will remain constant, may suddenly crumble around us. And what do we have left? Do we just stop living?"

He gave her a sad, twisted smile. "Something to ponder," he threw over his shoulder as he walked away.

Despite her initial reluctance, the little mermaid found that she enjoyed the Uncle's company more than she expected. There was a certain easy confidence about him, she decided, that the Prince did not possess. She did not feel like she had to perform, nor was she obliged to remove the scowl from his face, because he rarely scowled. In fact, all the little behaviours the Prince indulged in – moodiness, surliness, occasional mild tantrums, things that caused the mermaid to panic and rack her brain for ways to distract him – did not exist. However, this did not make up for the fact that the Prince was missed, and sorely. She thought his temper dangerously exciting, and his moods a welcome part of his mystique.

During the Prince's absence, she had at least learned a great deal. She had examined every corner of the city, even entering dress shops where the Uncle had indulged her by buying the small copper bracelets she admired so much. She wore them at all times and they jangled together when she moved. They had returned to the church and afterwards, the Uncle had explained to her all about the sad man, but the mermaid still did not understand what that had to do with anything. She desperately wanted to know about the Immortal Soul, but no amount of miming could persuade the King's brother into understanding.

The other positive thing, the mermaid decided, about the Prince's horrid journey was that it gave her the opportunity to return to the steps that led to the sea to soothe her bleeding feet. She had longed to spend time in the magic smatterings of dusk, but ached for her sisters and for news. She sat there for a long time every night, searching the horizon, but they never came. Questions started to form in her mind, and a horrible anxiety oozed into her heart. She prayed with all her might that her family was safe. She scooped up the sea-foam in her hands and kissed it, for it may be her sisters or their beloved nanny she held onto.

One night, sitting on a step with her feet comfortably lodged underwater in cool, slimy moss, a familiar sound wafted down to her from the high turrets of the palace. It was the haunting, terrible music that had imprisoned her so long ago and her heart began to race. Instantly, she was on her feet and running, her wet hem clinging to her ankles and copper bracelets jangling. She followed the music as she clambered up the floors, sometimes finding herself in empty rooms and courtyards, on the verge of hysteria when the music stopped. But the music would always begin again, and with her stomach in a sick, twisted ball centring her entire body, she burst onto a balcony and there he was.

He had his back to her, and under his chin rested a beautiful instrument of gleaming wood. He stroked its sorrowful strings with an elegant tapered bow, and the music caused her body to become racked with pain. She approached him slowly, and from an angle, she saw the artful slope of his jaw as it nursed the instrument. She began to run toward him, and as her body slammed into his, the instrument flew from his hands in surprise. As it landed on the ground there was a sound of wood crack-ing. But they didn't care. He kissed her fiercely, his hands grasping both sides of her face so tightly her head was sure to explode. Their bodies wound themselves together and they became fused with that moment in time. As the ocean roared beneath them and the stars cast their silly, useless light, the little mermaid tasted pain and deprava-tion and something sickeningly salty. She sucked all of it right out of him.

After a very long time, when they had both run out

of air, the little mermaid released herself and took a deep breath, staring at the face of her beloved. Her breathing soon turned into a gasp and a cold fist clenched her insides. She pushed him away with a violence she did not know she possessed.

"Why are you so angry?" said his beautiful, honeyed voice, and she launched herself at him and slapped him across his cheek. It was then and only then, did she realise her mistake: for the parasite that had lived on his face was gone. Her palm tingled from the smoothness of his skin, and even in the weak light, she could make out her handprint on his bare cheek. "Did you really think I was him?"

She shook her head, not in disagreement but in disbelief, for the man standing before her was so much like her Prince, yet so different. Suddenly she understood the hankering of the maids, and the female laughter beyond his closed doors. In a split-second, she imagined herself in his bed, being kissed like moments before, undressing and doing all of those unspeakable things the Personal Maid had divulged. And she had thought it all impossible then. The area between her legs felt strange.

"Is it this that's upsetting you?" he put a hand up to his face. "It's only been shaved. I thought it was high time. It can grow back, you know. Is that what you want?"

And the little mermaid shook her head so furiously that the Uncle laughed, which made the girl even angrier. *I... hate... your... animal!* she mouthed, and he read her lips and laughed.

"Animal? This? It's called a beard, and it is made of hair. Men grow hair on their faces just like women grow hair on their…" and his voice trailed off, and he glanced down the mermaids body impertinently.

But the little mermaid did not understand the innuendo, and her eyes began to sting mysteriously. The Uncle reached for her, but she wrenched away from his touch and turned her back to him, staring at the ocean and trying to draw a line between this man and the man she loved.

"I haven't kissed anyone like that," came the Uncle's voice from behind her, "since my wife. I was married once," he continued, "and we were happy. We lived here in this palace. We had a little daughter. But the kingdom was at war so I sent them away to an isolated village far from here to protect them. They were due to attack the palace from the water at any time. But their army did not begin here. They came across the back of the country, and they murdered and pillaged every town, every village they came across. My wife's was one of them.

"They never found her body. I wanted to believe that she was captured, so I left and I searched for her for a long time. It was an unhappy mission, because in my heart I knew she was dead, and it was all for nothing. They found my daughter's body. They brought it back to me, but by that time, it was old and decaying, half-eaten by dogs. But I held my girl in my arms until they forced me to let go and that stench did not leave me for years.

"And now, this mute girl from nowhere enters my life and everything changes. You know enough about our people now to understand when a man is offering himself to you. Don't let me resort to begging."

As much as she was moved with pity for him, she could not betray her love for the Prince. For he was the true reason her tongue was sliced out, not this second-hand man before her. Her certainty was so strong that nothing could persuade her otherwise. Yet why did she hesitate? The Uncle saw her battle and said, "You're not really in love with him, you know. You just imagine you are."

The statement was like a paper cut that severed her whole body, right from left. In a red rage, she pushed him away from her and marched toward the doorway.

"Why are you really angry?" called his infuriating voice after her. "The fact that you kissed *me*, or because it was *my* music that brought you here?"

Many nights later, one of several fitful nights of doubt and illusion, the little mermaid awoke from a dissected sleep to a great commotion in the hallway. There were voices, many raised and excitable voices, and with a jolt she realised that one belonged to the man she'd been avoiding since the night on the balcony. There were footsteps, heavy and quick, and several people speaking at once, then silence again. Suddenly, the voices started up again, weighty opinions and indignant tones colliding harshly. The little mermaid slipped out of bed and opened her door a fraction.

As she peered out her heart leapt, for one of the people caught in the uproar was the Prince. He looked better than ever, but she noticed that his voice was not raised in anger, but excitement. He appeared weary, and his travelling clothes seemed to wilt against the heat of his body. The Uncle was standing opposite him, arms folded across his chest in challenge, glaring at his nephew. He looked positively furious. Surrounding them was a throng of court advisors, who revelled in making their opinions known, and were not reported to be shy.

Before she knew what she was happening, she had emerged from her chamber and entered the hallway. The men fell silent at the sight of the pale girl in a thin shift, and the ring of people loosened and began to slowly disperse. The Prince's eyes lit up when he saw her, and he smiled at her strangely. He tilted his head to the side a little awkwardly and said, "It's great news, isn't it?"

"Hardly," muttered the Uncle darkly. He would not glance in the mermaid's direction.

But the Prince did not advance toward her in greeting, but stood perfectly still. An odd expression crossed his features.

"Now is not the time," warned his Uncle in withering tones.

"When is it not the time for love?" replied the Prince, and he smiled – the biggest, queerest smile the mermaid had ever seen. His mouth reminded her of the peel of an orange, when it is pared with a knife into a long, spiral snake. She shuddered and her eyes grew wide with fear. And there, in his eye, a new light blazed like a beacon, the light she had been waiting for.

"Isn't it wonderful?" he repeated. "I'm getting married!" And from behind his back emerged a very plain, very neat and ordinary girl.

Fifteen
THE BLUSH

BROOKS OF SALT water seeped out of her eyes – stinging, saline liquid that tasted empty and left puddles on her skirt where her knees were drawn up to the head. Heavy mucous dribbled from her nose down her face and into the collar of her dress. Her heart was like a strong man who tethered all her internal parts to himself with ropes of steel, and he tugged relentlessly. Her body responded in jerks and quivers like a useless puppet.

After a long time, the strong man grew tired, and the little mermaid wiped her face with the hem of her skirt. Her vision was blurred, so she rubbed the last of the salt water from her eyes with her fingertips and examined them.

"They're called tears," came a familiar voice. "They are exuded by glands around the eye when one is in extreme emotional distress."

The little mermaid had searched for sanctuary in one

of the upper balconies, for she knew her Personal Maid would be tidying the chamber and did not want to share her grief. It was shameful, this feeling inside. So this was what it meant to fail. This was why human lives were so short. The Great Condition. Sorrow, fear, agony and heartbreak.

So she stared at the last living relation of the man who had betrayed her, who was intruding upon her most humiliating, most desolate of days, then turned her head away with a deliberate haughtiness. Her face was crumpled like an ill-gotten love note, and the light that usually blazed in her eyes had been snuffed out.

"There's no need to be embarrassed," he continued, nonplussed, "they're quite common really." And the impudent man sat down beside her without invitation and crossed his long legs. He gazed up at the sky like the world had not shattered, like life had not just ended.

Exasperated, the molten tears returned and spilled down her cheeks. Mortified, she brushed them away wildly.

"They'll stop eventually," said the Uncle observantly, "You won't be crying forever. And you certainly won't feel like this forever."

But the little mermaid shook her head savagely. Of course she would feel like this forever. Everything she had sacrificed had been for nothing. She could kiss her Immortal Soul goodbye, but she was denied the chance to do the same with the Prince. He had found the girl, a girl that you and I would pass every day on the street without a second glance, and he was going to give her what rightfully belonged to the mermaid. Desperate to push the Uncle away and scream obscenities at his good intentions, she recalled an image: of a broken father holding a corpse in his arms. She bit her lip until it bled.

"It's always the last thing people want to hear at these times, but it really isn't so bad. You will find someone else, someone better. It always stings, the loss of first love."

But the little mermaid gave him a scornful look, for first love equalled only love, as merfolk are not acquainted with the idea of multiple partners. And it should be clear to the Uncle that there was no man on God's earth better than the Prince. God. That glowing orb in the sky, that stupid, unnecessary ball of gas that only disappeared as the world became darker. God was a coward. He was not watching, he was not protecting, he had no great plans. He probably did not exist after all.

The Uncle was not a man to be intimidated by girlish impudence, and he persevered. "Sometimes when we watch something from afar, it can seem so perfect. We crave that thing simply because we cannot have it. Instantly, it gains an exoticism. Finally, when we see it face-to-face, we realise that this thing we have worshipped and idolised for so long is riddled with flaws. We were just too far away to see it clearly.

"You know that I am referring to my nephew. It is hard to complain about his outsides, but it is his insides that trouble me. It has also kept you up many nights, even if you care to deny it." A cloud passed over his features and he braced himself against an invisible unpleasantness. "Perhaps you should go now. No, not to your room," he murmured as she leapt to her feet, desperate to escape his company. "To your world. Your people are sure to be missing you."

And the little mermaid's mouth hung open, like a door with a broken hinge, and she looked at this man who had skirted the realms of her petty existence, and realised he pivoted upon its very axis.

"I know who you are. I am not a man who has remained indoors, obscured by the certainties of his singular existence. I have travelled the world. I have listened to tales and fables, and I have seen phenomenons unfold before my eyes. And I've learned a few things chasing the dragon, as it draws back the curtains of my limitations to show me what lies beyond. I know all about you and your kind. I know how your species began - with a single wish, granted by the beings."

An old terror gripped the little mermaid and she remembered the darkness of the gorge and her abhorrence of what lay beneath. Their faces, their single, unanimous face swam before her eyes, although she had never seen them. But she could hear their voice upon the wind, their legion of whispering boons.

"I saw you, you know. Every night. Swimming up to his chambers and watching for him through the window. And when he wasn't there, I would feel such pity for you. So I played for you, and you would smile. And I would watch you and be gratified."

Suddenly, a series of events fell into place. The neat pile of maid's uniform at the top of the stairs. A bodiless chuckle. The instant introduction into the Upper Housekeeper's regiment. The gilt-edged card placed on her bed. The wardrobe of fine second-hand gowns, just her size. And worst of all, the mismatched flowers that had never passed through the hand of the Prince. She felt a white rage enter her, and the sensation of invisible faces surrounded her – laughing, laughing.

Ha ha ha ha ha ha. Ha ha ha ha ha ha ha ha.

In a burst of temper, she lunged at the Uncle. She hated him in that instant, for he had deceived her and pulled down the curtains of her reality. He had left her with nothing. But he caught her wrists before they flayed into him, and roughly wrenched them behind her back. "You have hit me once," he breathed into her ear, "but never again. You do not lash out at people because you are in pain. Do you understand me?"

Remorse filled her and she nodded. He immediately released her, but did not recover his distance. "Just because you sacrificed your life for him does not mean he must love you in return. He owes you nothing. It's part of the human condition. It's called *free will*."

And to his great surprise, the mermaid reached up and wrapped her arms around his neck, pressing her face into his chest. She could hear the pounding of his heart – wild, ferocious, like he had swallowed the animal that had once lived on his face. But he resisted her and backed away, unlocking her arms from around him. "No," he said gently, "not like this. Not like a consolation prize."

"When you are ready," he concluded, turning to leave, "I will be waiting for you."

After he had gone, she imagined this man rising before the rest of the palace every Tuesday morning to avoid detection. She could see him in the courtyard, selecting each individual flower, mismatched, no two alike. It was because he had known who she was all along, she who had never beheld flowers, and wished for her that pleasure.

It seemed the Prince, in his prenuptial joy, had completely overlooked sending the little mermaid an invitation to dinner. So she sat in her chamber, once so massive and ornate, now slowly closing in around her like a dark, damp cell. She rocked slowly, her hands pressed against the cavity between her breasts, wondering when her heart would break and thus, the moment that she should die. A double-edged sword had entered her side, a sword that bore unrequited love on its right and death on its left, and the little mermaid did not know which was sharper. Surely her heart would break at any moment. She wondered if a dramatic sign from the elements would mark the occasion – a flash of lightening perhaps, or a rock slide from the limestone cliffs. Perhaps the orange grove would burst into flames. The thought gratified her more that she would admit. But maybe there was more pain to come. The little mermaid shuddered. Any more was sure to kill her.

A trail of human regret left its crumbs along the progression of her thoughts, for she had begun to wish that she had never laid eyes on the Prince and that she had never saved him. She thought of his pale body, restrained by self-tied ropes, sinking beneath the water. Perhaps it would have been better to have left him there to drown, she thought savagely. And suddenly, the hard, cold beauty of the sea-witch swam before her eyes, and she remembered her words: "The person you're most like is…me", and repented of her thoughts. For she would rather die than share a bond with that vile creature. She wondered what the sea-witch was doing now, if she were watching her through a crystal ball, like the hired entertainers at the palace, with their shawls and drooping jowls. Perhaps her Sirens were with her, reporting the new events, and the sea-witch and her undeserved Immortal Soul were dancing a frenzied jig of victory.

But she was wrong on all counts. For the sea-witch had mostly forgotten her, and her beloved Sirens were dead.

There was a knock on the door, and the Personal Maid entered the chamber, bearing a tray of dinner and a baleful expression. "I've heard the news," she whispered, and she dumped the tray unceremoniously on the bed, and sat down beside the little mermaid. She rested a hand tentatively on the girl's back and rubbed gently. "I'm so sorry."

The little mermaid was all out of tears, and her eyes were small and bruised in her sallow, slack face. So she gave an ironic smile.

"I've just seen her, you know. Down the hall. Timid little thing, reminds me of a door-mouse. Won't look anyone in the eye, spends all her time in her room. Probably getting ready for the wedding, no doubt...not that I know when that is," she added hastily, seeing the mermaid's forlorn expression.

"I don't know what he sees in her. We were all pulling for you. You're so beautiful it was no wonder he took a fancy to you. But the Prince has always been, well, odd. What attracts most men does not attract him. He prefers the opposite. It's funny, almost like he means to show everyone he's different."

The little mermaid clenched her fists and squeezed tightly, until her nails dug into her flesh. The hands that had pulled him away from death and into the arms of the ordinary, rodent-like creature, she thought unkindly.

"Don't you worry, miss. There'll be a settlement for sure. He'll send you away, they always do, but he'll give you a gift: jewels maybe, and even a manor house if he really liked you. You'll never have to serve again. You're lucky really."

But she took no comfort in her words, and buried her face in her skirts. "You really loved him, didn't you?" asked the maid, and stroked her hair. The little mermaid nodded fiercely.

"There'll be another man. There always is. And you'll love him more, and forget all about the Prince. Don't shake your head like that, it's true. Our hearts are fragile and they break sometimes, but they're strong too and mend themselves in time. That's why we live as long as we do. If we all died of a broken heart, why, none of us would ever live past sweet sixteen!"

The little mermaid shrugged, for the words were nothing but prattle, white noise against a burning heart. She wondered where the Prince was now. If he had his ordinary girl backed up against a wall. One hand on her shoulder, restraining her, the other supporting his weight. If he was kissing her, if he was inserting his tongue into her mouth, washing it with the taste of olives.

"What about the Uncle?" asked the Maid pertinently, and the little mermaid jerked back to the present. "I told you I was loyal, and I meant it too. Anyone else stealing the affections of that man, and I'd claw her eyes out! By God, he's something else. And I hear he's got an eye for you. More of an eye, if the Upper Housekeeper is anything to go by. I say take the Uncle, miss. He's about twice the man the Prince is, if you get my meaning," and she winked at the mermaid like a rakish sailor, rescuing the lopsided tray and setting it down on the floor. "Now eat!"

Tension, like dust particles, fell from the sky and coated the inhabitants of the dining hall until they resembled stiff old museum relics. The Prince ate heartily, often stealing glances at his bride-to-be, who was seated opposite him. When she caught his gaze, she would smile shyly, but her eyes would always slide to the man on her left, who returned her stare with eyebrows knitted together.

"I don't understand the rush," began the Uncle. "You want to be married in one week's time. Unless you've already made her pregnant."

The Prince spluttered in his soup. "No Uncle," he said firmly, recovering himself. "There hasn't…well… there's been none of that, thank you very much. Unlike some of us," he added, with more venom than necessary, "who have a different chambermaid in our rooms every evening."

The Uncle eyed him sceptically. "I don't believe," he began coolly, "you have any right to comment on my preferred form of entertainment. It displays a lack of propriety. What would your father say to hear you talking like that? And besides, my boy, I gave up those sorts of dalliances long ago. But then again, you've been to absorbed to notice."

The Prince flushed, and the girl stared at her plate as if she had done something terribly wrong.

"Why not wait a year?" continued the Uncle amiably, as if nothing had happened. "Make arrangements, invite foreign diplomats, have elaborate wedding-clothes made, command a fleet of naval ships. Let the entire continent know we withhold no expense for the wedding of our monarch. Let us throw it in their faces. So what if we didn't choose one of their princesses, eh? We could even accompany it with your coronation, if you wish."

The Prince and the girl shared a look and he cleared his throat before he responded, "No, Uncle. We wish to have a small, quiet wedding here at the palace."

The Uncle frowned. "People will talk. They'll say you've acted inappropriately. That there's a bastard on the way."

"They will understand, in due time, that there is not," said the Prince carelessly, while his future bride blushed scarlet.

It was the blush that offended the Uncle the most. It was not that she was possibly the most unremarkable female he'd ever laid eyes upon, but that she was here, and the mermaid was not. He thought of the hot tears that had seeped into his jacket from where her face was crushed into his chest. The time he fell into the shadows when he saw his nephew kissing her – the clumsy fumblings of a greenhorn. He recalled his well-laid plans, his concealed encouragements for his nephew to be united with his companion. He had assumed that the Prince would fall in love with the mermaid simply because he himself had. She was a gold mine and the Prince was a blind mole, scratching at walls for something he was too befuddled to remember.

The Uncle didn't want the mermaid to have given up her life for nothing. And he would have been content to remain her benefactor, concealing his own feelings, nursing the fragments of his own heart on the familiar trail to nowhere. But here the Prince was, smitten like a clubbed mullet over a virginal child from a French convent. A child with a centre part so perfectly placed down the middle of her head, like it had been separated by a needle. A child whose excuses for breasts were aided by clever corsetry. In his opinion, this girl had nothing worth blushing over.

"Then they will say she had a miscarriage. Or that you ordered a physician to have the bastard killed. I know how these things work," he warned.

"Uncle, your language!" protested the Prince as the girl flinched.

"I am curious," continued the Uncle, pushing his plate aside and leaning closer toward the Prince, "how did you two meet?"

"I told you, Uncle," replied his nephew, shifting uncomfortably in his seat, "at the convent."

"Yes, I know the location," retorted the Uncle impatiently, "but not the details. I want the details." And he forced what he considered to be a welcoming smile.

The Prince looked at the ordinary girl and saw that she was anything but ordinary. His eyes lit up and his expression bloomed and he smiled at her beautifully. "The truth is," he began, "she saved me."

"From the ocean? After you *escaped* from the *foreign assassins*? Did she dive in, uniform and all? Or did she commandeer a ship with a crew of nuns and then fished you out of the water with a net?"

"Not like that," said the Prince softly, "but she saved me."

"Enlighten me," his Uncle demanded.

"The last thing I knew, I was bound and sinking in the water. And when I opened my eyes, she was there."

"So it had to be her."

"Yes."

"I'm curious," said the Uncle, turning to the girl, "is it in the Catholic education's curriculum to teach a young lady of means how to swim? Did the nuns instruct you themselves in their bare legs? Tell me, do they still wear their wimples in the water?"

The plain girl did not answer, and looked to the Prince for help.

"Can you swim?" inquired the Uncle, gently this time.

But the girl would not look at him, and stared at the Prince beseechingly.

"Can you even talk? Or are we to have the pleasure of another dumb maid's company?"

"That's enough, Uncle! You will not heckle her like this. Of course she can talk and will do so when there is something worth saying."

"Then let it be now, and let me hear from her own lips whether she can swim or not."

After a moment, the neat and tidy girl stared at the table and shook her head.

"I thought not," he responded, satisfied. "So if she did not rescue you from drowning, I wonder who did." And all of his meaning was lost on the pair, for they had caught sight of each other again, and had entered into a secret world of retreat.

"Of course," continued the Uncle slyly, "the kingdom was under the impression that you were to marry another."

The ordinary girl looked up sharply at this news. "Whoever could you mean?" asked the Prince in a bored tone.

"Your companion, of course. Don't you remember her? The beautiful foundling you've barely let out of your sight the last few months. Perhaps I should refresh your memory: library at eleven, courtyard gardens at one, horse-riding at four, dinner and dancing in the evenings. And then you would walk her to her chambers, and sometimes instead of merely saying goodnight, you would..."

He trailed off deliberately, hoping the Prince would cut in, blazing with self-righteous protectiveness for his new chattel. But instead, he seemed to slump into his chair, and a scowl began to flicker over his features.

"I think she was under that impression too," continued the Uncle in gently. The Prince buried his face in his hands and sighed deeply.

The silence was only broken when the kitchen staff wheeled in a tray of desserts. To his great surprise, the bride-to-be suddenly applauded enthusiastically and seemed to bounce in her seat. "Orange tart!" she exclaimed in heavily-accented tones, "My favourite!"

It took six days for the Prince to summon the courage to broach the little mermaid. He actively avoided her all week, sending his servants on missions to discover her whereabouts, and once they had reported back, confining himself to the opposite end of the palace. He sneaked about the palace at night, jumping at the sound of footsteps, believing it to be her. He took to joining his Uncle in the opium den to simply calm his frayed nerves. Yet every time a woman came toward him, his heart would begin to race, and his armpits would exude sticky sap that slid down his ribs. And even though it was a blatant insult, he did not once invite her to dine.

In these six days, the Prince discovered he did not like confrontation, especially when he was in the wrong. He dreaded the coming discussion and yet greatly longed for it, as he hoped it would expunge the cinders of guilt that marred the otherwise happy times spent with his future bride. His companion's face would swim before his bride's, like a death mask. The taste of fish pervaded his bride's saliva, and it reminded him of her.

He disliked the flat remarks his Uncle would make on the subject, but did not retaliate as he was wise enough to know they were well-deserved. And so he wrote a speech, a long-winded missive of justification and proposed absolution which he carried at all times upon his person. He imagined her response – tears, to be sure, begging, perhaps – all in all, a scene. He wondered how any man could look into the love-crusted eyes of a woman and say the words, "I don't love you."

He took his chance at sunset, the day before the wedding. A servant had informed him that the mermaid was last seen at the unused staircase that led to the sea. Why anyone would venture down there, he had no idea. But it was isolated, so it would do. He ran shaking fingers through his unruly hair and examined his face in the looking-glass. Chasing the dragon had left chalky grey rings around his eyes. Then, clenching the speech in his fist, he ran from the room.

His pace only slowed when he was halfway down the staircase, the moss causing his heavy boots to slide dangerously. He gripped the handrail and looked upon the slumped back of his companion, her shoes strewn beside her, her feet in the water. He did not want to go further.

"Hello there," he called lamely, "Do you think you could come up here?"

Without surprise or recognition, she quietly gathered her things and mounted the stairs, each step searing through her like she were treading on a sea of nails. Slowly she made her way to the step he was resigned to, and stopped, her arms slack at her side, a shoe in each hand.

"I've been meaning to talk to you for quite some time now," he gushed. His voice sounded harsh. He did not know how he could soften it. It was just pouring out of him. One look at her face and his conscience was jabbing him in the ribcage. "As you know, I am getting married in the morning. We have had a – a –" He fumbled with the paper and unfolded it, forgetting his place already. As he was about to state the words 'appropriate companionable friendship', a sudden gust of wind took hold of the speech and blew it far away, over the horizon. The Prince and the mermaid watched sadly as the paper flew out of sight. There was a long, funeral silence. They kept standing on the wet step, awkwardly.

Before her could examine them in his mind, unscripted words had already dribbled from his lips. "Why do you love me?" he asked sadly, not really a question, because the answer did not matter to him. "I am not worthy of your love. You don't know me or my inmost thoughts. If you did, you would loathe me, I am sure."

The little mermaid shook her head firmly. She wanted to say that she had learned of suicide, and understood sadness now and still she had wanted to take it away from him. That there were parallels between them, solid, concrete parallels that would always exist and why couldn't he see that? She wanted to plead with him to choose her, not just for love, but because she would soon be dead if he did not. But life without his love would be like death anyway, and it was hopeless. She wanted to say that he had cheated her. That the sea-witch had cheated her. That her father and her nanny and her sisters had all cheated her, because they never told her the truth. Of course, she could not say these words. So she stood there quietly, feeling her heart pealing slowly in her chest, wondering when it would break. Then he said something that truly surprised her.

"I don't know who you are, or where you have come from. I don't know how, but I believe you were there the night I nearly drowned. I think I saw your face looking down on me. And I think I felt your skin on my skin. So thank you."

The sick shadow of gladness filled her. He had finally discovered the truth! He had to love her now! He was going to send the girl back to the convent and he would marry her instead. But her gladness dissolved as he continued, "I have sheltered you and befriended you for the last months. You have had the best of all things. My Uncle and I have arranged a house and a generous living for you. Consider my debt repaid."

The little mermaid hung her head in humiliation. There was such shame for the empty hope and trust in the schemes of the fiery orb overhead, which she now realised was nothing but the sun. Shame that the only reward for love was a structure that would decay and a handful of coins that would be spent on a few pretty dresses and a fistful of copper bracelets. Worthless.

"You will be notified of the arrangements. Goodbye," he added and turned away hastily. But the mermaid was not ready to be flung aside so quickly, and she grasped his wrist firmly.

"Now what?" cried the Prince gruffly. "What is it you want? Have I not given you enough? If you ask me, it is love that destroys things. As much as it brings goodness, as it has for me, it also brings devastation. Some people can't take it. It decays them. It's so wonderful in the beginning, and then turns sour, like oranges I am too stuffed to eat. Look what it is doing to you! Your love for me, what has it brought you in the end?

"I'm not going to tell you that I love you, even if it is what you want. But I do. It is not the kind of love you want from me. My love for you will never satisfy. I told you before, I never had a friend until you. So if you still want my love, if that kind of love is good enough for you, then you will take the house and in time, you will attend all of the palace functions like a dutiful subject, and you will pretend that you loved me the same way as my little black dog."

And in the last act of affection, the Prince seized her hand and kissed it gallantly. He was gone before the sun set and all she could hear was the sound of a violin, when it clattered to the floor.

Sixteen
THE END OF THE END

THE REMAINING PRINCESSES had come to the end of their tether. The deaths of their three younger sisters had flung them into action that their calm, small minds had never thought possible. Gone were their voracious appetites for heavy feasting, because the kingdom's hunters had either died of the unknown virus, or lost the necessary limbs in exchange for the Finfolk's expensive tonic that claimed to slow the disease, but could not cure it. The princesses neither lingered in front of their looking-glasses, because their beauty had diminished rapidly as the disease spread its fingers through their bloodstreams.

After they previously and unsuccessfully visited their sister on land, who did not return with them, they had been at a loss once more, yet strangely relieved to be parted with her company. For there was something about her face that repelled the princesses with every contortion, and it fed the virus inside them. The third sister replayed those facial expressions in her mind all day long, until she finally curled into a tight ball and dissolved into foam before their eyes, the terrible drumming a crescendo into silence. More reports of death had reached the palace, and it was estimated that more than half the merfolk population had either died, or were on the verge of death. No one bothered to shop or eat anymore. Even their father, who had seemed so strong and immortal, complained of splitting headaches and restricted his movements to the perimeters of the palace.

After exhausting the boundaries of their limited imaginations, the two eldest princesses took their very last chance. Taking a lacklustre group of their strongest guardians and leaving their sense behind, they ventured outside the protection of the palace. Over the sleeping city they swam, muffled cries of pain and numerals carried in the current. Over the abundant oyster farms, the molluscs yawning to reveal their opulent treasure, with no one to harvest it. Over the barren wastelands and the great, sunken graveyard where a lone gypsy watched from a rig with his one good eye. They were not disturbed by the ear-splitting screeches of the plants with faces, who wavered in their garden as if in a frenzy. They did not rest until they were deep inside the cave of the sea-witch.

There was no glint in her eye as she welcomed them in. Most of her beauty, the eldest thought, was gone.

The Prince and his ordinary bride were quietly wed in the orange grove one fine morning. Much to the mermaid's disappointment, the grove had not been set alight, its white trees like skeletons amidst the harsh daylight. A string quartet played traditional melancholy tunes, and members of the court milled about mournfully, finding their seats. The fat Countess sat near the front, and wondered whether a mousy thing like that could grant the Prince the physical pleasures he truly deserved. The physician that had attended to the mermaid sat in the middle, and privately rejoiced that his majesty had not married someone with such horrid dental structure. The Personal Maid peered down from where she was jostling overhead to the storage chamber with an armful of rich robes, and shook her head sadly.

The King's brother stood up for the Prince, gave his blessing, and signed the necessary papers. The newly-married couple turned toward their audience and beamed, but the audience did not beam back. They arose from their seats in a dignified manner, and filled their bellies with orange tart and tea. The Uncle walked among them, sullen and downcast.

The little mermaid was not invited, but she was there nonetheless, hidden in the shadows of the surrounding balconies. The Uncle knew she was watching, but the rest of the court assumed she was packing her things, although she owned nothing of which to take, excepting some copper bracelets and bag of dried flowers. The court did not know what to make of the sudden turn of events. But even the most resistant of women had decided in the mermaid's favour, simply because they did not believe a plain girl deserved the love of a prince.

The Uncle had tried in vain to persuade the little mermaid to accept the gift of his late wife's clothes and jewellery. She had shaken her head firmly, staring down at the box of glinting stones, blinking at her like oblivious eyes. She had also refused to view the manor house recently purchased for her, an extravagant complex with a household of trained servants, a well-stocked stable and a feed barn. The mermaid had not sealed herself inside her chambers as expected, but spent most of the day and night upon the old steps at the back of the castle. Sometimes, the Uncle would watch her silently from the upper balconies, her shoulders slumped, hair flying tangled in the wind. It occurred to him that she may simply give up on the human race and return to the depths. So be it, he thought, there is nothing I can do. So he tried to relieve her with music, retrieving his second violin and beginning to play. But when he glanced down to gauge her reaction, the little mermaid was standing up, fists clenched at her sides, glaring up at the turrets. He hastily dropped the bow.

But if she decided to stay, the Uncle was sure she had particular uncertainties that plagued her, as did all females, no matter the species, such as occupation, companionship and livelihood. He was determined she should be a lady of leisure, and hoped to acquaint her with the entire repertoire of leisurely pursuits. Then he planned to marry her. For he was a man who had suffered loss, and in turn, was entitled to take whatever was offered, sometimes more, from the women around him. But he had made a deal with God, if God existed at all, and knew that the outcome would prove just that.

The King's brother was many things, but he was no fool. He convinced himself that the mermaid felt the pangs of unrequited puppy-love for the boy, and in time, she would forget him. He knew there was something between them, something built from sweat and fire and warring bones, and he was determined to chase it. No woman had warmed his bed since the Prince had gone in search of his bride, and he had vowed that no one but the mermaid would do. At nights, sucking down his nightmares with an opium pipe, the drug would induce unblemished visions of their future together, and the Uncle imagined it was God's way of sending his blessing.

The mermaid sighed and her entire body slumped against the railings as she watched the Prince kiss his bride shyly from where they were seated at the ornate banquet table. Her heart thumped away merrily inside her chest, as if it had never known sadness and desolation. Wretched thing, thought the mermaid, wondering how much time remained. Over the past weeks, possibilities had run through her mind, chances that he might change his mind, that he may look closely at his bride and see she was just as plain as the half-breed mares in the stable. Even now, there was still time for an annulment. But the little mermaid found she was either too exhausted or too complacent to wish for such a thing.

She watched them indistinctly, like shadow puppets moving against a blank canvas, for she was aware that too much detail would hurt. She now knew it had all been in vain. It had never been her, because all this time, the fetid stench of oranges had filled the Prince's mind and heart. After he had returned with his bride, he had not only forgotten her, but revoked all his prior affections and intimacies, treating her with a callous indifference. It was like she had never existed. She would not forget the cold, disjointed way he had bid her goodbye, dumping the responsibility of creating her a living on his Uncle. The ungrateful boy knew that she had saved her and still he washed his hands of her. Well, he was sure to make a horrible husband and an even worse king. And he was right, the kind of love he was offering her was not enough. It had no value at all.

Defeated, she left the wedding party to their merriment and wandered slowly down the empty halls. Melancholy ghosts reached out for her with their translucent fingers, but she slid right by. The Prince's traitorous black dog spotted her in the lower floors and gambolled to her side, but the little mermaid fended it off with her foot and hurried onwards. She stopped when she reached the old staircase that led to the sea.

The stone steps were hot to the touch in the midday heat, and she shielded her eyes from the glare that turned all things white. Flying-fish squawked and dove beneath the shining waters, ready for their luncheon, clacking hungry beaks. She could barely make out the grand wedding ship, docked at the end of the pier, waiting to take the couple on their honeymoon tour that very afternoon. She wished she had a rock to throw at it. A rock large enough to sink the vessel. She wished she had a sword to flay the mast in two. There seemed to be an abundance of white sea-foam that coated the ocean, and some lapped onto her feet before disintegrating into nothingness.

Dozing off in the haze of anger and heat, she dreamed of a black sea, thick and murky like tar. Against the blackness, something was pulsating, something darker than the oil surrounding it. Suddenly, it pushed its face against hers, and the mermaid beheld the sad eyes of the sea-witch, and they looked just like her own. The witch was all alone, just another ink blob in a sea of ink.

The little mermaid did not wake until she heard voices calling her name. They were familiar, like they belonged in her dream, but rasping and dry, as if issued from a mouth with no saliva. Hands pulled at her ankles and wrists until she woke with a start, and screamed a long, terrified, silent cry. For there before her were two spectres, each with one eye gouged out, teeth pulled from their bloody gums and gills sawn from their necks. The hands that grasped her ankles had only two fingers left on each, and all their hair was shorn.

"Sister!" one hissed, and the little mermaid recognised her and wept, but no tears came out. Just dry, wracking sobs.

The princesses regarded her blankly, the strange twisting of her face. It no longer bothered them, like it did before. It was no longer so strange, so displaced.

"It is us, youngest sister!" wheezed the eldest princess. "You must come home with us. For the sea-witch told us your mission has failed. You have nothing left here."

The little mermaid shook her head and pointed to her legs. The second-eldest opened her mouth to reveal black gums. "We have given all but our lives to the sea-witch and exchange for this. It is your way out." And with her two claw-like fingers, she held out a silver dagger, its handle ornately carved into the head of a serpent. The little mermaid reached for it and caressed it. It felt warm and familiar to her.

"Everyone is dying, sister," coughed the eldest princess

through globs of blood. "All the gypsies are dead. Most of the commoners too, they are perishing with every passing moment. Our father is taken ill. Even the Sirens have been dead these two days. Only the sea-witch seems immune. You must return home at once and help us."

But the little mermaid gestured wildly and shook her head savagely to indicate she did not know what to do. In response, the sisters did a surprising thing. They grasped her hands and slammed them to their bare, withered breasts. She could feel the pulse of a creature beneath each hand, awake and hammering and hungry. Her stomach flipped inside her. "You have always been different," said the eldest with her grey, vacant stare, "return home and help us."

"When no one is watching," hissed the second sister, "creep onto the wedding ship and conceal yourself there. Wait until midnight, when the moon is high in the sky. Then enter the Prince's chamber and as he sleeps, plunge the dagger into his beating heart. When his blood splashes onto your feet, you will become one of us again."

"Make haste!" croaked the eldest, "for the party is about to board the ship! Go now and we will ride with you, and wait below you for your return!"

The little mermaid froze and stared at her sisters imploringly.

"We will go with you," said the sisters reassuringly. "We will be waiting. You have our word."

The little mermaid nodded, for she could not argue, and jumped to her feet. But before she ran toward the pier, she took both of her sisters' faces between her hands and kissed them soundly on the lips. They looked at her with their singular empty eyes, and she scampered away.

Balled up between crates of expensive French wine in the hold of the wedding vessel, the little mermaid was alone with her thoughts. She spent the hours until midnight pondering many things, and listening to a voice inside her asking blatant questions, many of which she had no answer. She grieved for her people and all of her sisters and prayed in vain for her father, likening him to the man in the stained-glass pictures who walked willingly to his death. But her father's heart was stone-cold, and he had no Immortal Soul to carry him to heaven. So she turned the dagger over and over in her hand, trying to summon the strength to carry out what she was bid, all the while ignoring the voice that sought to reason with her.

After all, she could return home and forget that she ever knew humanity or tasted loss. She would be clever and conniving, like the Personal Maid had described, and return to the sea-witch. She would outplay her at her own game and demand an antidote for the foul disease. Perhaps she could be persuaded to give up her hair or an arm in payment. What good were they to her now? Perhaps she could save the merfolk, all of them.

And in the dark hold of the honeymoon ship, the little mermaid discovered that she, like any other mortal creature, was terrified of dying. A deep survival instinct ignited within her and she desperately wished to spare her own life, no matter the cost.

Logically, she planned the deed in her mind. Removing herself from crates, she crept around the hold, examining the stairs and the planks of the ceiling. She built a careful tower of boxes, and fumbled her way to the top, where she pressed her ear against the ceiling and listened. After a great deal of time and discomfort, the little mermaid discovered where the bridal chamber lay and the whereabouts of the royal servant's compartments.

From above her, a beloved voice drifted through the cracks.

"Pay them no mind, my dear," said the Prince, in a tone so gentle that the mermaid was uncertain of its owner, for just a moment. "They are a fickle people but they will come around. You are my Queen now, and their Queen also."

The ordinary girl replied, but her accent was so thick and unfamiliar that the little mermaid could not fathom her words.

"I think," said the Prince in that strange tone, "that you are beautiful. And anyone who cannot see that is surely blind."

Despite herself, the little mermaid half-smiled. She had not realised the Prince was capable of uttering such endearments. Suddenly feeling ashamed of eavesdropping on newlyweds alone in their bedchamber and discouraged by the pain in her neck, she quietly began to dismount the boxes. But instantly, she froze still. For there was a sigh of desire and a rustling of silk, the groaning of a feather mattress. She listened unashamed to the rattle of bed springs, the hammering of the master board against the wall. There were human whispers too, and restrained, hidden moans. The little mermaid gripped the boxes to ensure her balance. Splinters invaded her fingertips, unnoticed. The place between her legs felt strange but she was fascinated and listened until the final, guttural whimper and the collapse of two bodies onto the protesting bed.

Like a puppy who has taken too much dinner, the little mermaid retreated to her hole between the champagne crates and buried her face in her knees.

Suddenly, there was a loud noise and light filled the darkness. The trap door had been flung open and someone from the deck was descending the wooden stairs into the hold. The little mermaid pressed herself flat against the crates and edged her cloak closer around her body. She was too frightened to turn her head to see who this intruder was, but the sound of his voice told her everything.

"You haven't seen a girl, or anyone for that matter, come down here?" demanded the Uncle, waving a lantern to illuminate the dark corners of the space.

The sailor, clutching his hat in his hands, replied sheepishly, "No, your lordship. We've been on deck all afternoon and never saw a soul come down this way. Nasty place for a girl, if you ask me. Spiders and rats and God-knows-what-else down here."

The Uncle said nothing and ventured into the maze of crates. "Has…has someone gone missing, your lordship?" inquired the sailor sheepishly, trotting after him.

"Stay here," he commanded, and disappeared amongst the crates. Slowly he walked down the dusty floorboards, following a pair of fresh footprints embedded in the thick dust that coated the floor. They stopped before a nest of crates. The Uncle kneeled silently upon the ground and reached a hand into the black hole, grasping the little mermaid's forearm. He swung the lantern over to behold her horrified face and opened his mouth in reprimand.

But the girl's expression froze him in his tracks. Her eyes were beseeching him and she was breathily heavily, frightened that he should give her away. The Uncle had little idea of what she meant by skulking about in the dark, but realised she was not coming back. Suddenly, God retreated back to his cloud and did not bother him again, and as far as the Uncle was concerned, his son remained nailed to his cross. And so, despite his better judgement and the wisdom of his years, he closed his mouth and released the mermaid's arm. The last he saw of her were the whites of her eyes.

The moon rose in the sky and the servants fell quiet. The footsteps up and down the deck ceased and there came the sound of several doors closing for the night. The vessel halted and the great anchor was lowered, allowing the captain to retire to his quarters. The mermaid lay on the floor for one hour and waited, making sure every soul on board was asleep.

Slowly and cautiously, she alighted the wooden stairs that led her to the deck. She pushed open the trapdoor and winced as the hinges gave a squeal of protest. Frozen, she waited for someone to become alerted and rush to capture her, but there was nothing but silence. After a long moment, she hoisted herself out of the trapdoor and lightly stepped onto the deck. Grasping the dagger in her hand, she looked up at the moon that soaked her with its pale milk. It was almost time.

She crept slowly to the entrance of the ship's largest

chamber. She placed a hand tentatively on the doorknob, fearing it locked. But as she turned it slowly, the catch easily slid out of its groove, and pushed open silently. A strange medley of smells greeted her, sweat and other bodily omissions, perfume and flowers. Scented wax from candles. Sexual heat from underpants.

Tiptoeing to the enormous canopied bed, the little mermaid held the dagger poised as she peered through the gauze curtains that had been drawn over the couple, rustling gently in the breeze. She parted the sheer material as quickly as she could and looked down upon the outline of the sleeping Prince, his head turned toward her.

This is justice, she told herself fiercely. I gave up my life for him. Now it is his turn. Justice.

She sucked in her breath and summoned all of her courage, and as she was about to plunge the weapon downwards, the moon suddenly moved and flooded the chamber with its light.

As she beheld the Prince, engulfed in the warm arms of sleep, she was struck anew by his unmarred beauty. But his beauty seemed enhanced by an expression she had never seen before. It was one that conveyed the deepest peace and utter contentment. It was what he had failed to conjure from his own blood, cutting his flesh with the self-same dagger. It was contentment that she could never have given him, because that occupation always belonged to another.

Instantly, the little mermaid realised she wasn't angry anymore. She wasn't disappointed and she wasn't sad. She envisioned the future King on the throne, ruling his people with a kind and firm hand, his neat and tidy Queen by his side, and she smiled. She imagined their children, little princes and princesses, running about the halls she had become so familiar with, playing with the ghosts. She felt a sense of wonder at her imaginings, and a warm gratefulness filled her that she could have tasted his life, and even held a small place in his heart.

The Prince shifted in his sleep and whispered something. For one wild moment, the mermaid imagined it was her own name. But it was the name of his bride, the girl he lay beside, and once again he was still in his sleep. The parallels that she had nurtured and relied upon, constructed from ignorance and daydreams, cracked and fell to the floor.

Tenderly, the little mermaid reached out and traced the line of his brow with her fingertips. Her fingers fell over his lips that had once so entranced her and his smooth angular jaw. She would not forget the way he explored her mouth, searching for answers. She would not forget that hair could fall like that.

Knowing what had to be done, the little mermaid left the chamber and closed the door gently behind her. She made her way to the railings of the deck, and looked out over the still emerald sea. With one perfect movement, she pitched the dagger into the ocean, where it became lost amidst the depths, never to be recovered. And without a second thought, she hurled herself over the edge.

They say your life flashes before your eyes upon the moment of your death. But for our heroine, it was as if her life as a mermaid had not existed, for all she saw were images of the human world. As she relived every moment in those last futile, eternal minutes, a sickeningly salty taste flooded her mouth and the sound of a mourning violin filled her ears.

A face arose in her memory, a care-worn, brutal, beloved face and suddenly, her arms began to move and her legs began to kick and her body yearned for the surface. Hope filled her and she smelled his skin upon her own and she could taste a lifetime held in this man's arms.

It came to her, suspended like a pendulum in the whispering water, that she had been deceived. As the pale luminescence of the moon shattered beneath the clear water, tracing fractured patterns over her skin, she remembered the God who was coming in the morning, who had planned for her to be there. Different and set apart from the moment of her birth, the little mermaid finally realised that she did not have to wed the Prince to gain an Immortal Soul – that she had her own all along. She did not know how it was possible, but surely humanity had been hers from the beginning, as she had recognised the fluttering weight of her soul from the moment of her birth. The knowledge flooded her with warmth and her heart continued its slow, steady beat as if it had known the truth all this time. Filled with joy, she clambered with all her might for the surface, as her lungs were constricting with lack of air and black shadows merged on the edge of her consciousness.

But as she struggled in the water, sinking further into the depths, the little mermaid remembered that in her human form, she had not learned how to swim. She began to panic as water gradually filled her mouth and lungs. Her vision blurred and became black, and all the joy, hope and love she ever felt shut down, like a theatre after closing night. And as she comprehended the consequence of this one stupid, minute detail in the progress of her life, she finally experienced humanity's Great Condition. Enveloped in the coldest sorrow, her heart broke in pieces and ceased its fateful beating. The ocean swallowed her up and she drowned.

Epilogue

J UST AS LOVE had birthed it, it was love that eliminated the race of merfolk in the end.

Her remaining sisters would have said that she was
beautiful in death, floating to the ocean floor like a lost
feather of a flying-fish. It need not have happened at all. If
they had been present, as promised, beneath the depths of
the wedding ship, they would have caught the little mermaid in their arms and brought her to shore. Her lungs
would have expanded with air and gratefulness as they
hoisted her onto the stone steps. She would have run into
the palace and to the man who loved her, who had done
everything in his power to prove it. She would have married him and produced one olive-skinned son with ring-
lets and a hot temper. They would have grown old, hides
like crisp, dry leaves, and their graves would have been
dug side-by-side in the royal cemetery. Her sisters could

have prevented her untimely death, had they not died themselves sometime between midday and midnight.

Every dead heart in the underwater kingdom had been awakened, and the dreaded word festered amongst the merfolk until their minds blew open from too many thoughts, and their hearts exploded from too many beats. The disease became so advanced that even the tiniest flare of light in an eye would cause the toxins to be transmitted from one to another. Even the unborn, seemingly safe in their eggs, became infected, their tiny dead hearts snapping inside them. The Sea King himself, the strongest of all, was the last to die, gazing out of his window at the eerily still kingdom, remembering his wife.

The only trace now left of the species is the mother of all merfolk, who began the race with a broken heart and a boon. She wanders amidst the empty ruins and shells of old ships, aimless and bored. Even the beings refuse to admit her, tired of requests they have not the power to grant. She tries to kill herself twice a year but the bargain will not allow her. She is still there now, an eternal phantom, fruitlessly trying to abandon her Immortal Soul which follows her about like a mocking spectre. Sometimes she becomes so desperate for companionship that she comes to visit me, with her dry tears and empty lament. Usually, I pretend to be nothing but the ruins of an old lighthouse and she soon leaves me be.

Lately, she stays longer, as if she has realised that I have ears and all I can do is listen. She talks endlessly of days gone by, recalling the glory and the greatness of her creation. About a man I vaguely remember, and a basket of red tomatoes. She mourns her beloved Sirens, the most perfect of creatures, and asks me if I think she will have the strength to one day create again.

But most of all, she talks about a daughter she once had, who she initially despised as the offspring of one who betrayed her. How the beings bought the baby's life, and in exchange had granted her the opportunity to choose the child's form and time of birth. How she had waited countless years and plotted an intricate plan, beginning with the slaying of the Sea King's useless, bled-out wife. The assurance that the girl's true heritage would eventually upset the delicate balance of animal and human, lending to its ruin. How she greatly longed for the destruction of the merfolk, and how her broken heart had deceived her. It had whispered promises to her in the blackest of nights, none of which came true.

She feels regret now in her old age. She often wonders what could have been had she not deceived her daughter, if she had aided her just a little. If she had first used the girl for her own purposes, but afterwards released her to her own human right to life.

Call me a fool, but I believe her to be genuine. She still wears a braided necklace of her daughter's hair around her neck. I imagine her sometimes, discovering the corpse on the ocean floor. I wonder if her heart stopped, just for a moment, like an ordinary person. But it probably went on beating as usual, as if nothing momentous had occurred. I wonder what she did with the body, whether she buried it humanely or if she ground the bones into a poultice and swallowed it down in an attempt to keep her daughter within. My eyesight grows weaker and I cannot see as far into her cave, you see, so I must dream up these things.

As for the little mermaid, I like to imagine her a happier end. I sometimes envision her own Immortal Soul rising from the grey dawn of death and bursting through the surface of the ocean, golden and perfectly whole. She travels toward the magnificent palace of glass and limestone where she lightly kisses the new King and Queen of the land. Then she enters the bedchamber of the King's Uncle and spends one night beside him, resting against his beaten, second-hand body. All around him are neatly packed bags containing his possessions, waiting to leave in the morning. She whispers and caresses him until he falls asleep.

Now, I know I am just a lighthouse, a man-made structure and a ruined one at that, who knows nothing of religion and science like you do. But I imagine her then travelling toward the great light of heaven. And as her soul flies up into the clouds, the God himself is waiting to greet her. He holds out his arms and she runs inside them. He touches her face and says, "I know your name."

Splendid gates open wide, and he disappears inside them into the golden city beyond. She smiles and follows.

ACKNOWLEDGEMENTS

DROWN HAS BEEN a long, long journey. The story has been with me for over a decade and its publication not only fills me with pride, but a deep sense of relief. It's like unloading a burden you've been carrying around for ages, or delivering a baby you've been pregnant with for ten years.

Firstly, I would like to thank Holly Root of Waxman and Leavell Literary Agency, who was not only my very first agent, but the first person to believe in *Drown* professionally. Thank you for all your work, rewriting strategies, and long meetings with all those editors. You were the first person to make me think, "Hey, maybe this could be a career". That alone has helped me through many a long, barren night.

I wouldn't be where I am now without the support of my parents in my formative years, always pushing me to write and finding me special tutors to encourage my ability. To my brothers, who looked over my shoulder at the screen of our family dinosaur of a computer, laughing at every sentence I wrote and teasing me mercilessly: thanks for preparing me for the critics. And to my grandfather, who is himself an author, thank you for inspiring me from the time I learned to read, and praising to heaven my childish poetry and adventure stories, though they were greatly unworthy of such accolades or attention. I carry your opinion of my abilities into adulthood, and subsequently, this novel.

To my husband, for doing the laundry, feeding the baby, smiling through the stress, the PMS, being yelled at for interrupting my train of thought, many apologies and twice as many thanks.

Is it futile to thank a famous dead man? Hans Christian Andersen, who wrote the original fairy tale *The Little Mermaid*, birthing whilst simultaneously horrifying generations upon generations of fans, I hope I have stayed true to the spirit of your allegory, which is the one element of this novel that I would not compromise.

And finally, to my daughter, who inspired me before she could even speak a word.

ABOUT THE AUTHOR

ESTHER DALSENO WAS raised in Australia and the United States.

After leaving Sydney in 2007, she decided to live abroad for one year, teaching English in South Korea. She never returned.

Esther has also lived in Laos, Vietnam and Thailand and has travelled the world extensively. Along the way she acquired a husband, a daughter, and a Pekingese dog.

This strange menagerie now live in Berlin.

Esther Dalseno was previously published in the acclaimed short story collection *We All Need a Witness* by Pan Macmillan.

Drown is her first novel.

CPSIA information can be obtained at www.ICGtesting.com
Printed in the USA
LVOW11s2203101115

461894LV00004B/416/P